FLY, FLY AWAY

Also by Pamela Bauer Mueller

THE KISKA TRILOGY
The Bumpedy Road
Rain City Cats
Eight Paws to Georgia

Hello, Goodbye, I Love You
Aloha Crossing

HISTORICAL NOVELS
Neptune's Honor
An Angry Drum Echoed
Splendid Isolation
Water To My Soul
Lady Unveiled
A Shadow of Hope

FLY, FLY AWAY

Pamela Bauer Mueller

PIÑATA PUBLISHING

Piñata Publishing
626 Old Plantation Road
Jekyll Island, GA 31527
(912) 635-9402
www.pinatapub.com

Library of Congress Control Number:2019945320

ISBN 978-0-9809163-6-2

Cover art by Gini Steele
Typeset by Vancouver Desktop Publishing Centre
Printed and bound in the United States by Cushing-Malloy, Inc.

I dedicate this book to all the Pedro Pan families, whose leap of faith gave their children hope, freedom and new lives. Thank you for your courage.

Taste and see that the Lord is good; blessed is the man who takes refuge in him.

—Psalms 34:8

There is no greater agony than bearing an untold story inside you.

—Maya Angelou,
"I Know Why The Caged Bird Sings"

AUTHOR'S NOTE

An author friend once told me, "If you get an idea for a story, try to forget it, and if you can't, start writing."

I first heard about the Pedro Pan children from an immigration attorney. As I listened to her explain what the Pedro Pan program had accomplished, who were swept up in the largest exodus ever of unaccompanied children in the Western Hemisphere, and the heartbreaking choice their parents had been forced to make . . . I got goosebumps.

When she ended her narrative with: "*Yo soy Pedro Pan* (I am a Peter Pan child)," my eyes filled with tears.

Her story was intense and exhilarating. I had spent ten days visiting Cuba and eighteen years living in Mexico, without ever hearing this complex, epic tale. When she asked me to consider writing a novel to share with the world, I agreed to think about it.

There would be so many challenges to face. I'm not Cuban and I'm not a Pedro Pan. Some who experienced it first-hand had already published memoirs or well-researched documents about the exodus. I had just finished writing a novel, and I really needed a break. But I couldn't get the story out of my head.

It took me a year to finally say "Yes." I eagerly began my research and planned a visit to Miami to meet a few Pedro Pans.

The personal adventure of exploring the unknown has always been a visceral motivation for me to write. This story had been told, but not from the perspective of someone outside looking in. And I knew I'd be putting a big part of myself in the characters.

History is a conversation between the past and the present. Depicting characters with careful attention to detail and lots of heart is the novelist's prerogative and obligation. I try to explore the emotional center of my work—to remain vulnerable and truthful. By immersing myself into this overlooked slice of history, I came to appreciate the lessons for all of us in these children's turbulent lives.

Writing is an act of faith. You must believe that a story's details will reveal themselves to you as needed. I knew I wanted each central character to be a composite of several real Pedro Pans. I never used their real names, their photos or other identifiers. I read many of their books, and was able to interview a few of them. Their stories helped me to write my story while respecting their privacy.

Every historical event in this book is factual. Each personal story shared with me was enhanced with tales from my imagination. The four main juvenile characters came from my head and my heart. The journeys described here all happened to the real Pedro Pans. Because this is a work of historical fiction, it introduces important players who are real people: Father Walsh, James Baker, George Guarch, Padre Palá, Polita and Ramón Grau, and others.

The "truth or fiction" question inevitably arises. Readers will wonder what I imagined, and what events actually occurred. The answer is simple: my task as an author is to craft emotional truths about characters' relationships—the reasons the characters do what they do. Inner lives can only be explored in novels, not history books. As a historical novelist, the most fulfilling feedback comes from readers who are inspired to do more research into the events and the characters' lives after reading the novel. This is what historical fiction does best.

I am so thankful to my Savior for granting me His presence as I walk with readers through this story. The greatest gift I have received is His grace.

PROLOGUE

September 14, 1963

Today is my fifteenth birthday. In Cuba, my native country, the *Quinceañera* is a huge celebration for young women turning fifteen as they become adults. It is a very exciting social event, and is comparable to a "Debutante Ball."

And as I become an adult in the United States, the birthday gift I'm giving myself is the celebration of my freedom. I will also celebrate by sharing my story with you. This story is taken from my diary, which I started writing when I was twelve and leaving Cuba. It has become a part of an important milestone in American and Cuban history. My brother Diego and I were swept up in the Western Hemisphere's largest ever exodus of unaccompanied children. The responsibility we bore broke many spirits and almost destroyed our family. But freedom and a brighter future are worth fighting for.

This epic story began unfolding when I was twelve, and Diego only seven. But I'm telling it now through a fifteen-year-old's voice, because I could not have written it earlier. Now I share it, with all the courage, discipline and strength I received from my family. With their encouragement I feel ready to open my heart and soul to unveil the story of two Cuban children who joined a mass movement of Pedro Pan children in response to Cuba's social upheaval.

The story is not only about us. It's also a love story involving our parents, because so many Pedro Pan parents had to make the heart-wrenching decision to send their beloved children to the United States without them. And it's a story of survival, as innocent children were forced to learn how to live without surrendering their culture and traditions.

I have finally found a peaceful place, where I can enjoy my memories and build a better future, filled with hope, faith and love.

PART ONE

Liliana & Diego

1

April 21, 1961

Just after dawn, my parents silently entered my bedroom. I still heard them. "Today is the day," Mami whispered, lowering herself to the edge of my bed. Her face was framed by the window, where the new day was sprouting colors of promise.

I sat up and looked over at my special canvas duffle bag leaning against the wall. The day before we had packed my limited wardrobe: three dresses, three blouses, two pairs of pants, three pairs of socks and underwear, one sweater, one set of pajamas and one book.

Papi once again reminded me that there was a weight restriction on every suitcase, and if you were even one ounce above it, they would make you leave behind one piece of clothing.

"That's what a Revolution is all about: ounces," he grumbled under his breath.

"Where's Diego? Is he up and dressed?" I wondered.

Mami nodded as she handed the new yellow checkered dress my grandmother made me for this trip. Last year *Abuelita* (Grandma) gave me a gold ring she had worn as a young lady, which I have never taken off.

I turned around to rescue Olguita from my pillow. She was the only doll I still had and looked well-worn. Mami told me I would be allowed to take her with me. I had slept with her since I was five years old and needed to have something personal and comforting with me, even though I no longer played with dolls.

I gazed at my father. His handsome face was exhausted and haggard, his clothes wrinkled and grey. Sadness seemed to be hanging over him. He handed me a paper he had prepared, with my and Diego's names and our Cuban phone number. He told us we would be met at the Miami Airport by a man named George in Miami.

"Papi, who is George?" I asked again. I had forgotten what he told me just the day before.

My father smiled and pulled me in close for a hug. "*Preciosa*, I'm not sure. When someone from Father Walsh's organization meets you, you just ask for George." He pinned the paper on my dress. "You must be very brave, Liliana. This will be just a temporary separation, but you must take care of your younger brother Diego." His smile wavered as tears formed in his eyes.

The sky was still a pale pink as we drove to the airport. Nobody spoke. I felt a sense of hopelessness that I couldn't understand. Our school had told us that we would receive a *beca* (scholarship) to study in a good school in the U.S. I was excited to fly on an airplane, but worried about the secrecy surrounding our journey. We could tell no one that Diego and I were leaving except for my grandmother. Not even my cousins knew.

My mother turned around and rested her arm on the front seat. "Remember to use your manners. The people who will help you deserve your respect. Say please and thank you, and remember to bathe every day."

Her familiar instructions took me back to our last shopping trip together. I had argued with her because I wanted to buy a pair of low heels that she said were impractical for this trip. "This may be the last time we shop together and you're going to fight with me and deny my final wish?" I whined. Mami shook her head, chuckling fondly. I wore those shoes on this trip so I would feel more grown up.

There were only two daily flights to Miami, and we were taking the afternoon one. My parents had been given instructions by the Cuban authorities to be at the airport at a certain time.

Inside the airport terminal, I noticed the black and white pattern on the tile floor, looking like a huge checkerboard. A large wall mural at the end of the terminal was captioned *Say Yes to the Revolution.* Women were crying and hugging their children goodbye. I felt my knees quiver as I walked behind my parents, holding my doll Olguita close to my chest.

We saw the *pecera* (fishbowl) ahead: an all-glass enclosure with a high ceiling.

Mami told us that my brother and I would be entering the departure area and then stay together until the flight departed, perhaps several hours later.

"We'll be able to see you through the enclosure until you board the plane, "Papi said solemnly. "We'll all be back together in a few months at the most," he assured us. We stood around for a long while with other anxious families, and I looked around to see if I knew any other children traveling alone. Diego and I didn't recognize anybody.

Finally it was time, so our parents started hugging us, holding us as tightly as they could. My father again told us, "We'll all be together in a few months. The U.S. won't allow this to continue much longer. They will get rid of Fidel." I watched him blink back bitter tears.

Diego clutched Mami's hands. "I won't go. I don't want

to." Papi gently loosened his grip and nodded at me to step forward. We walked slowly, but both of us turned around a few times to look back at them. I needed to memorize their faces, their bodies, their clothes. Mami smiled at me and reassured us that they would wait until our plane left. The last image I had of my mother was of her hands reaching out toward us, as if pleading for us to come back. I took a step toward her, let out a sob, and then turned around, heading away from her toward our uncertain future.

We moved through the guarded door and had to wait where the others traveling on visa waivers were huddled. Finally, two soldiers—a bearded man and a short woman—called us all forward. We watched, alarmed, as two young women came out of a back room in tears.

The lady soldier spoke loudly. "Listen up, everyone. We are doing random searches for items that are illegal to take out of the country. We will select every fifth person to come with us to make sure that you are not removing any of Cuba's riches. If you are trying to smuggle anything, you will need to turn it over to us now." Both soldiers were dressed in army fatigues and seemed proud to be holding rifles with bullets, while ignoring our obvious despair. Neither of us was number five, so we were ordered to move forward to the baggage inspection line.

I looked at the window separating us from those behind the glass. I saw Mami's tear-stained face. She lovingly mouthed the words, "I am here."

"Diego, are you ready?" He nodded silently. I took his hand and we walked to the baggage inspection and watched as the soldiers poured out the contents of our duffle bags onto a large table. When they saw we had exactly what we were told to pack, they left us to separate our belongings from the other children's, and repack them. It was then that I noticed a small book I hadn't put inside the bag—an autograph book. I opened it and read: *This book is for recording your personal thoughts and your new adventures. We will enjoy reading it together when we join you in the United States.*

Dear Mami, I thought tenderly. Somehow she'd found a way to sneak it into my duffel bag.

Suddenly the woman soldier turned around and frowned. "Give me your doll. Perhaps you are hiding jewels or money inside her."

I handed Olguita over and watched the soldier roughly prod her arms and legs. Finding nothing, she tossed her back to me. "Wait one moment," she growled. "Is that a gold ring on your finger?"

"Sí, Señora. It's my grandmother's ring." I answered her cautiously, feeling an unexpected sense of dread.

"Hand it over to me. It belongs to Cuba. You were already told not to take anything belonging to the Revolutionary State with you," she scowled. I removed it, and she grabbed it with an unfriendly smirk. I struggled to hide the pain of this cruel loss.

Diego was wide-eyed. "Why did you take away her ring?" he blurted out. "It's Grandma's ring, not the State's." I pushed him forward before she could tell us to get out of her sight or do something worse.

"Let's move on, Diego," I told him, motioning him forward.

"She took your ring, Lili. She can't do that."

"Shh, little brother. Let's see if we can see Mami and Papi through the glass wall."

We finally squeezed into a small place against the glass wall. We spread our open palms against the glass, hoping our parents could see us. They did, and hurried to put their palms directly across from ours through the thick enclosure. We repeated *"Te quiero"* (I love you) again and again, never taking our eyes off each other. Finally our boarding announcement was made, and we had to move onto the plane.

Holding tightly to Diego's hand, I walked backwards to keep my eyes locked on our parents. It was so painful watching them disappear from sight. I felt like my life was ending. My heart ached, and my mind seemed ready to explode.

Diego took the window seat. I was not interested in looking out, but when Diego tugged on my arm and pointed upward, I could see a small crowd of people huddled together on the rooftop observation deck. I needed to have one last look. I saw Mami standing proud, waving a white handkerchief. Papi just stood next to her, looking overwhelmed with loss, his head down and his arms hanging loosely by his side. I watched them as the plane taxied down the runway, and I felt my heart split in half. Seeing them grow smaller and smaller, I kept watching as they became indistinguishable from the disappearing island of Cuba.

A sense of hopelessness overpowered me as I listened to the crying children in the cabin. I closed my eyes as we rolled forward.

"Lili, I don't feel good. My tummy hurts me," whimpered Diego. I squeezed his fingers and gave him the bag in the seat pocket.

"I'm going to throw up, Lil," he moaned, as the plane picked up speed, pushing me back into my seat. His little body shuddered and heaved as he emptied the contents of his stomach into the bag. The wheels left the ground, and we rushed into the sky. I rubbed Diego's back as he lay collapsed across his seat with his head in my lap.

We were up in the air for the first time, no longer on Cuban soil. We were aloft, like Peter Pan and Tinkerbell. The sun was setting, glowing with mandarin orange and mango colors. It made a brilliant reflection, streaming across the water as far as the distant horizon. But it wasn't setting where I always saw it before. The sea seemed bigger than I could have ever imagined, but there were no waves. It looked dark blue, not turquoise as usual. Cotton clouds were everywhere. I saw Havana's high-rise buildings towering over Cuba's rugged landscape.

Emotions choked my throat as I whispered *Adiós, mi preciosa tierra, mi Cuba.*

2

April 21, 1961

Father Walsh was worried. *I'm just a bundle of nerves today*, he thought ruefully, lightly running his fingers through his hair. As an Irishman, his eyes were bright and curious, which some compared to a leprechaun.

His early morning prayers had already been interrupted by several telephone calls. He stood up and headed for the front door, ready to stretch his legs before the sun scorched the already humid morning.

A soft knock at the door reached him halfway across the room. James Baker was poised to knock again.

Father Walsh smiled. "Greetings, James. I was about to take a walk to clear my mind. Care to join me?"

James nodded. He could see that his friend was agitated. He could use a walk too. He hadn't found enough time to exercise recently, and it was beginning to show.

"Tell me, Bryan. Have you been up a while?"

"I couldn't sleep much, James. It's about the children. So many are arriving weekly and we simply don't have enough homes for them." He paused, searching James' eyes for answers.

"Let's walk over to the diner and get some breakfast. It's easier to brainstorm over a cup of coffee." Father Walsh nodded mutely, worry shadowing his eyes as they strolled across the diner's parking lot.

The friends had first met on December 12, 1960. In less than a year and a half, working as a team, they had been able to bring between seven to eight hundred unaccompanied Cuban children into Miami. Since the previous week's Bay of Pigs failed operation, the demand for visa waivers had drastically increased.

After ordering breakfast, Father Walsh brought his cup of coffee to his lips and blew on it pensively. James waited for him to collect his thoughts.

"You know I have the authority to grant visa waivers to the children aged six to sixteen," he began. "And have granted quite a few lately. So our lists have become longer than we can now handle."

James recognized his friend's reluctance to get to the point. "But we still have the funds to get them into foster homes, right?"

"Yes, but there are no more foster homes available in Miami, or even in the rest of Florida. We'll need to send them to homes and even orphanages in the other states. We need more assistance here to manage that." He sent James an odd look, full of apprehension.

"Are you referring to more workers, Bryan? I can find you more Cubans and priests to help us if you just say the word." James reached over to cover Father Walsh's free hand with his. "You know our network is large."

The priest nodded wearily, prompting James to think about how reluctant Father Walsh was to ask for financial help. Their constant need to find new supporters had taken its toll. The priest seemed to be aging prematurely. He was only thirty-two.

They chatted about their families and light-hearted

small talk about friends. Once their plates had been cleared away, James decided to broach the complex subject with a touch of wry humor.

"Do you remember when we thought we'd only have about two hundred children arriving from Cuba? It all seemed much easier then, didn't it?"

"Yes, our biggest worry was keeping the program under the radar of the Cuban regime. And we have, at least for a while," he said, a bit emotionally as he folded a paper napkin into small squares.

"What? Do you think Castro knows now? Have you heard something?"

"Nothing definitive, but some of the priests' contacts in Cuba are nervous that he no longer will allow Cubans to leave the country. Apparently his Revolutionaries are starting to turn back Cuban professionals and technicians at the airport. Fidel seems to be afraid of this program creating a serious brain drain for Cuba."

Gazing directly at James, he cleared his throat and opened his hands imploringly. "Guide me, my friend. I feel helpless and I'm unsure why."

James studied his face for any show of desperation. He was at a momentary loss for words.

"Bryan," James reminded his partner, "let's try to remember that we've never been defeated so far. The Lord has not given us more than we can handle, nor will He ever. Remember when we needed proof that the children had been admitted to schools in the U.S.? We prayed, and several days later, Mrs. Agnes Ewald at the Coral Gables High School came forward and offered to provide us with those papers."

Father Walsh smiled broadly at the memory. "Praise God! We got them through safely in the Embassy's diplomatic pouches. And we brought over one hundred twenty-five minors through Agnes."

"Then what new potential do you see for our project?" James blurted out.

"I'm simply realizing that I, a Catholic priest, and you, a Protestant school teacher, have worked closely together for some time based primarily on our shared faith in God. As our work grows more extensive and the potential for political complications grows here and in Cuba, I think more people might become interested in our unique model and consider how it might be applied to other issues or movements.

"It's easy for people to get discouraged these days about complex international issues. Often they try to improve their process rather than gaining inspiration from a shared vision. We're demonstrating that no matter how large or hopeless a cause may seem, bringing good people of faith together to overcome a major problem can still accomplish a lot."

He smiled his self-deprecating half smile and began to look like his cheerful self again.

"In our case, we enlisted the help of the Catholic Welfare Bureau, the Children's Service Bureau for Protestant Children, and the Jewish Family and Children's Service. From the beginning, we agreed that the religious heritage of all the children would be safeguarded."

"And we've succeeded in that as well, haven't we Father Walsh?"

"Indeed we have, James. Indeed we have."

The sun was now beating down, and the heat was rising off the pavement. As they returned to Father Walsh's office, James felt a renewed lightness in his friend's mood.

"Why don't we contact Katherine at the Children's Bureau about our housing situation? Surely she will have some suggestions and perhaps find us more aid from the Social Security Department."

"What a great idea, James! Thank you for lifting my spirit," he said, relaxing somewhat. "Now I can thank God for what we will receive."

As he watched his friend return to his vehicle, Father Walsh was relieved that he had avoided burdening James with his primary worry. Since *Operation Pedro Pan's* inception, Father Walsh had asked the press not to report on the exodus of the unaccompanied Cuban children, as this might endanger their exit from Cuba. The media complied with that until shortly after President Kennedy's inauguration, when he gave a speech about helping them. The *New York Times* covered that speech in February, stating "President Kennedy has explained that his 9-point program will provide four million dollars to relief agencies, including financial aid for the care and protection of unaccompanied children—the most defenseless and troubled group among the refugee population."

So far, Father Walsh had heard no mention of any response from Fidel Castro's regime. No news was good news, he believed. But the apprehension still burrowed in his mind, and daily he prayed that his own inner peace and their broad-based support would overcome it.

3

April 21, 1961

I was awakened by the sound of children sobbing. Diego was twisted in his seat, fast asleep. My mind raced with crazy thoughts, and I struggled not to think about our uncertain situation. I concentrated on peaceful subjects, like music and movies. I wanted to believe that I was going to a place where no one would talk about the Revolution or Communism.

We were quickly descending for the landing, and moving to a country we had never visited. The beach rising up to meet us reminded me of Cuba, with its many palm trees. The turquoise/green water was like ours, and so was the white sand. But as we flew above the airport, the rest of Miami looked very different. The roads were lined up perfectly, and the buildings all seemed to be the same size. I didn't see any hills or mountains. This looked nothing like Havana.

Just an hour earlier we had been in Cuba with our parents. It felt so far away and such a long time ago. Soon we would be living in a country we didn't know. In less than an hour we had left our familiar life behind. My past seemed to be fading away minute by minute, and I was beginning to forget my world.

The plane's tires squealed as they hit the runway. Diego

woke up with a start and looked out the window, a hopeful smile growing on his face. He began chattering about our arrival.

"Liliana, are we here? Will George find us and take us to his home?"

I smiled tenderly at my seven-year-old brother. His new enthusiasm warmed my heart.

"Yes, we'll go find George. Then, who knows? Off to a new adventure!"

Diego tightly gripped my hand as we walked from the plane to the building. Once inside, we were surrounded by bright colors, happy people, and noise. It was so nice not to see guns or soldiers anywhere. People were speaking English so fast I couldn't understand them. This surprised me, since I had always received good marks in my school English classes.

I looked around and saw that most people on our flight were being greeted and hugged. We had no one expecting us, except maybe a man called George.

As we entered a wide room with lots of suitcases lined up, three older teenage boys from our flight asked us if we were waiting for George.

"Yes, we are," replied Diego. "Is one of you George?"

They all smiled. "No, we're waiting for him as well." Since they were Cubans, we communicated happily in Spanish. "Let's go find a place to wait for him to find us."

It didn't take very long. A well-dressed thin man approached us with a big friendly smile.

"Are you five *Cubanitos* looking for George?" he asked in Spanish.

"Yes," I quickly responded. "Do you know him?"

"*Yo soy George.* (I am George). Father Walsh sent me to pick you up. Welcome to Miami."

I felt so relieved. I heard kindness in his voice and saw it in his eyes. He spoke like a Cuban, so we all could continue speaking in Spanish.

"Let's get your bags, and then we'll find out where you're all going. As you know, the church has found you a place to stay, at least temporarily. I'll be taking you there."

As we picked up our duffel bags and headed outside, George led Diego aside. "Don't worry about a thing, *hijito* (little son), because you are safe here."

"Yes, my sister and I will be together and I'll be fine."

"Are you hungry?" he asked us. "Have you ever tasted a McDonald's burger and milkshake?"

We had not, so he drove us to the restaurant and ordered for all of us. This gave us time to get to know each other a little, and George kept up the cheerful mood during the meal, which was really good. This was our first meal in the United States, and we liked it very much.

"Now, first we'll go to the Kendall facility, and then to a different camp across the street. You older boys will go downtown, to the Cuban Home for Boys. I'll be dropping you off last."

Diego frowned. "Perdón, Señor George. I want to stay with my sister. She's supposed to take care of me on this trip."

George smiled a little nervously. "You will be right across the street from your sister. You'll see her almost every day," he reported.

Now I broke in. "Can't Diego and I stay together? I promised my parents I would watch over him." Everything shifted in my mood.

"They will explain everything to you when you get there. It's very well-organized and smoothly run."

Diego searched my face for reassurance and grabbed my hand. I squeezed his fingers and smiled with as much encouragement as I could.

There was plenty to look at while driving from the airport. The houses were larger and the palm trees seemed smaller than what we had in Havana. The street lights were very bright and we enjoyed seeing this new place.

Then the station wagon pulled up to the place that George said was the Kendall House. It looked like two large buildings separated by a small road. Later we were told it was a former army barracks turned into a camp. An older woman dressed in a long skirt and white blouse was waiting for us on the porch.

"Here you are, Miss Liliana Escobár," George said with a smile before we got out. "Let's go meet Señora Fuentes. Please let me carry your duffel inside."

Then he turned to Diego and pointed out the window. "Diego, please wait here for a moment. You will be staying across the street, at least until we can find a foster home for both of you."

Diego's eyes were filled with distress. "Don't leave me, Lil! You can't go without me!" He pulled on my arm to stop me from getting out of the car.

"Diego, don't be afraid. I'll be right here and will think of a way we can see each other every day."

"Liliana, he will be fine. He just needs a little time to get used to this new arrangement." I hugged my little brother and kissed him on the cheek.

"I'll see you tomorrow, Diego. Get some sleep. We must pray for Mami and Papi and for each other." My brother just sank into his seat without saying anything.

George led me to the porch and introduced me to Señora

Fuentes, a fellow Cuban. Then he shook my hand. "It was very nice to meet you, Liliana. You will be comfortable here, and I'll check on you both in a day or two."

I glanced back to see Diego staring defiantly at me through the window. When I waved he just turned his back to me. I blew him a kiss which he never saw.

Slowly, I bent down and picked up my duffel bag to follow Señora Fuentes inside. Poor Diego. I knew he was trying so hard to be brave.

As I followed Señora Fuentes inside, a wave of sadness swept over me.

She made small talk as we stopped in front of the first room down the narrow hallway.

"Do you want any milk or water before you go to bed?" she asked me politely.

"No thank you, Señora. George took us for hamburgers. Also, it's quite late now."

She showed me my upper bunk bed, just inside the door. Girls were asleep in the other beds so we whispered.

"Don't worry, dear. We always give the newest children the beds closest to the door, but as more girls arrive, you will be able to move further back and choose another bunk." She said it like it was a privilege.

I thanked her and quickly unpacked my few belongings. It was so quiet in here. Not one girl woke up as I unpacked. After washing my face and brushing my teeth in a shared bathroom halfway down the hall, I climbed into my bed. I began to pray but sleep overtook me. My Olguita slipped to the floor, and I was so tired I never heard her fall.

4

April 22, 1961

I woke up wondering where I was, startled by a bell ringing outside. I felt something warm beside me, and then saw the bed covers move. Opening my mouth to cry out, I felt a small hand grabbing my arm. "Be quiet, Lili. It's just me."

"Diego, what are you doing here?" I gasped.

He whispered a simple explanation. "I was scared over there, so I came over to your camp last night when I couldn't sleep."

"But how did you know where I was?"

He shrugged. "I walked to the first sleeping room with beds and there you were, so I climbed up to your bunk. We slept together all night," he answered with a giggle.

I quickly tossed the covers over his head. "Keep quiet, Diego. We'll be in so much trouble if someone finds you here." My mind whirled as I tried to figure out how to get him back to his camp without anyone noticing. I finally decided we'd make a run for it. After all, my bed was the closest one to the door.

Reaching for his hand, we snuck out silently as the others began to stir. Once outside, Diego began whining. "Please take me home, Liliana. I am so frightened over there by myself." He stopped and stood stiffly on the sidewalk, his body rigid and his hands clenched at his sides. Then I saw his eyes glassy with tears.

I wrapped my arms around him, and he burrowed deeper inside my embrace.

"Don't worry, Dieguito. You will be just fine," I assured him as I brought one hand under his chin and tilted his face toward mine. When he offered me a feeble grin, I took hold of his hand. "Now, let's take you back to your camp."

A priest met us at the door with a small smile. "Is this the new lad who arrived last night? You must be his sister. Thank you for returning him, just in time for breakfast."

I smiled gratefully and was turning to leave when he invited me for breakfast. "Join us for oatmeal and warm milk, and I'll let them know across the street that you're here." Diego's eyes opened wide in appreciation.

"Thank you, Father. I should love to join you all," I said, looking into his gentle blue eyes.

He led us to the large dining area. "You'll see each other again this afternoon, after classes have finished," he told us.

Again, Diego pulled on my arm. "We didn't even get into trouble," he whispered like a born conspirator. "I think I have a new friend."

I talked to him after breakfast. "Diego, we were lucky this time. Do not do this again. I'll figure out a way we can see each other, but we must follow their rules until that's possible."

He nodded silently.

"Diego, please tell me that you understand me."

"Yes I do, Lili. I will see you later. Please work on a plan to get us home."

I walked back to my camp. The sweet smell of daffodils rose from the damp earth to meet me. I choked on a sob growing in my chest. Señora Fuentes was waiting for me again. Instead of chastising me, she took me directly to English class. Of course, I was late.

"Gracias, Señora," I said timidly as I took the seat she indicated.

That day, I made my first friend at the lunch table. Her name was Estela. She quickly offered me her bottom bunk, since she would be leaving in a few days to live with a family in Ohio.

"Are you excited?" I wondered. I did not know where Ohio was.

She shrugged. "I don't know. It will be a new adventure. But I miss my family so much."

"Are you here alone?"

"Yes, my parents only sent me. They said my brothers were too young to come, at least for now." She hesitated, then smiled. "How about you?"

"My seven-year-old brother is across the street with the younger boys. He's so scared and only wants to go home."

I think she understood my anguish.

Estela smiled graciously, then asked me a question. "How old are you?"

"Almost thirteen," I told her. "But I'm supposed to keep an eye on Diego, and I can't if we are separated."

"Liliana, don't worry. You will see him most every day, when they send the younger ones over here to play."

"How old are you, Estela?"

"I'm already thirteen and will be fourteen in September."

"What day? My birthday is also in September!"

"September 9th. When is yours?"

"On September 14th I'll be thirteen. I hope to spend it with my parents, but that's now just a dream. I pray for that every day." She nodded her understanding.

I stopped talking, too shy to ask her when she thought her parents would arrive.

As if reading my mind, she nudged me and added, "Soon you two will be sent to a foster family as well, unless your parents come for you first."

I wondered what she meant, but decided to figure it out later.

Walking out to the central yard, I heard Diego's voice calling me. Then he was leaping into my arms. "Lili, do you have horrible food over here too?" Diego loved to talk about food.

I laughed out loud. "Not too bad, Diego. But let's wait a few days before we make our final judgment."

Sitting at a picnic table, I explained that this separation would not be easy for us, but we could hope for a reunion with Mami and Papi in a few weeks. In the meantime, we should focus on learning English, meeting new friends and praying that a nice family would be found for us until our parents arrived.

Diego's eyes remained troubled. "What if they separate us?" he whimpered.

"I won't allow it, so you can put that idea out of your head. I promised Mami and Papi."

He crossed his arms and pouted. "I know I'm not going to like the food here . . . ever."

"Hey little brother, let's go play a board game." To change the subject, I led him into the main hall. We played checkers for a while until they told us it was time to go into supper.

"Liliana, you brought your autograph book with you, didn't you?"

"Yes, Diego, you saw it in the airport. Why?"

"Tomorrow please bring it with you so I can see Mami and Papi's signatures. And yours and mine too. I just want to see it. It's all we have of them with us, isn't it?"

My eyes closed, feeling the tears squeezing out from under my lids. I quickly blinked them back.

"Of course I will, Diego. Now go back to your camp and then to bed—your own bunk bed—and I'll see you again tomorrow."

To my surprise, he stood up and walked slowly behind the other boys to his camp.

I went to supper, shaking my head as I tried to unravel my racing thoughts.

5

April 25, 1961

I fell apart on my fourth night at Camp Kendall. It had rained for two days so they didn't bring the boys over from across the street. I knew Diego would be upset and saddened at not seeing me. When I asked the house mother and one of the nuns if I could go over there, they both said "Not today."

I wondered where George was, since he'd told us he would check on us "in a day or two," but he hadn't come. Last night I cried myself to sleep, missing my parents and my life in Cuba so much. And I was not the only one. Every night I heard girls of all ages sobbing and crying out for their families, even in their sleep. It was so upsetting to hear. I wished we'd never come here, and I desperately wanted a phone call from my parents, like some of the other girls had received. I really needed to hear their voices.

Estela snuck across the room to comfort me when she heard me crying. Sitting on the edge of my bunk bed, she wrapped her arms around me and just let me cry. I gave in to my grief and loneliness, and after a moment, it seemed to help.

"Oh Estela, I'm so sorry," I whimpered, my voice catching on the words.

She looked at my swollen eyes, shaking her head.

"Liliana, don't apologize. Starting over is so hard, I know. Life has so many surprises, some of them good, but others that hurt very much." She paused, then added almost inaudibly, "I'm so sorry you are suffering."

"Thank you, Estela." I wiped at my eyes and took the handkerchief she offered. "We just met, but I will miss you. Please don't forget me when you leave."

"Of course not. And I'm still here another five days, so we have more time." Then she picked up Olguita and handed her to me. "I brought my doll too, but gave her to a little eight-year-old girl who forgot to bring hers." She smiled at the memory. "You'll feel much better in the morning." After another hug she tiptoed back to her bunk. I could already feel the tension slowly draining away from my body.

"See you in the morning. Thank you." As I fell asleep, I understood something my mother told me last year. Mami tried to explain life to me when my kitten went missing. "Hijita (*Little daughter*), I'm not asking you to forget her. This has nothing to do with forgetting. But nothing is ever so bad once you accept it." *Sí, Mami. I will accept this even though it hurts terribly.*

I woke up to a bright blue sky filled with sunshine. Sunlight flooded into the rooms from outside, reminding me of my home in Havana. I caught my breath at its sudden beauty, and smiled.

I thought I would see Diego today, and I did. When he and the other younger boys raced over to our patio after lunch, I was totally unprepared for what I saw.

His face was alive with excitement, his eyes dancing as we embraced.

"Dieguito, I've missed you. I'm so happy to see you," I

told him, laughing happily even when he quickly stepped away again.

"Lili, I couldn't come over. They kept us in but I know so much about making airplanes now. Father Menendez is so nice," he grinned cheerfully. "I'll show you what I made from a kit he gave all of us!"

His cheerful mood continued as he told me about his past two days. I was so relieved that he was no longer angry or sad. We sat at the picnic tables and played two board games, and I let him win. I wanted to keep him happy.

A tall man waved from the other side of the patio, putting out a cigarette as he walked toward us. I recognized him: It was George! He'd finally come here to see us!

"Hello Liliana and Diego!" he called to us while approaching. "How wonderful to see you together like this."

We greeted him with smiles. I was very happy to see him.

"We don't get to see each other every day, Señor George. In fact, today is the first time I've seen my brother in three days."

"Ay, yes. The weather has been terrible, right? But now we're back to our beautiful spring sunshine." His eyes lit up when he smiled.

"Diego, have you made some friends already?" he asked, responding to the huge smile.

Diego nodded eagerly. "My favorite person so far is Father Menendez, but I also have a couple of friends my own age," he acknowledged.

"And you, Señorita Liliana?"

I appreciated his interest. "Yes, one or two. But my new favorite friend is leaving in five days."

"Well, that's good news, right? And soon you and your brother will be going to a foster family, I hope."

"May I ask you some questions now that you are here?" I asked George, suddenly nervous. He paused intuitively, then withdrew a note from his coat pocket. He turned to Diego and asked him to please deliver it to the boys' side of the camp. I think he didn't want Diego to hear our conversation. How considerate!

I looked directly into his eyes. "First, I want to phone my parents. I've not heard from them since we've arrived. Do they have my number?"

"Yes, they do. We contacted them the day after your arrival. But you should know that it's difficult to get calls to and from Cuba because so many calls are being placed. It would be easier for them to phone you than for us to try to reach them."

I shrugged, realizing how helpless and needy I must look.

He leaned closer to me. "Please try to be patient, Liliana. I know they will call you as soon as they can."

Nodding, I continued. "Also, we were told we had been given a *beca* (scholarship) to study here. Where is it?"

George sighed. "We needed to use the *beca* terminology to get your visas. In the beginning, the children who left Cuba did attend boarding schools with those *becas,* but when so many of you applied, we simply couldn't find schools and families for all of you. That's why you are studying here to improve your English. Once you get a foster family, you can attend the local school near there."

I felt my lower lip quiver. "Señor George, that's my next question. How much longer will we be here at Kendall?"

"Hopefully we can get a family for you and Diego in the next few weeks. We're doing all we can to keep you two together, so it may take a little longer." His eyes seemed sad, making me feel badly for him.

"Also, I'd like to meet Father Walsh. I have more questions for him," I stated.

"I hope that will be possible. In the meantime, why not write him a letter that I will take him?" he responded. "He tries to meet every child, but it's become impossible with his heavy caseload. Can you understand that, Liliana?"

I nodded. "Yes, Señor. I'll write them down for you this evening." I smiled softly when I saw his unsettled expression.

"Then I can pick them up, since I'm bringing two sisters here tomorrow. I think one of them is twelve years old," he smiled. "Hopefully, I'll be here by nine in the evening, and you can hand me your questions and meet the two girls."

Later, we saw Diego return and run to join his new friends playing soccer. I felt a strong sense of gratitude. Perhaps God was watching over us, since I prayed for peace about our life here every day at morning Mass. I needed to remember to count my blessings this evening.

"Thank you so much. I hope to see you tomorrow night." I gave him my hand. He gave it a gentle squeeze and let me go.

"Have a grand day, and give Diego a hug for me."

"Goodbye, Sir. And thank you very much for answering my questions."

6

May 1, 1961

Dear Father Walsh,
My name is Liliana Escobár. I am almost thirteen years old now. I came here two weeks ago from Cuba with my little brother, Diego Escobár. We are living in two different sections of Camp Kendall and are separated by a road. We can't even see each other every day, which is a big problem. You see, when my parents sent us out of Cuba to keep us safe from Fidel Castro's communism, they made me promise to take care of Diego, who is only seven years old. He is frightened when he is away from me but also very homesick. So am I, but I don't tell him that because I have to be the strong one.

Señor George has been very kind to us, and he told me that I could write you with my questions. I have several, and each day I seem to think of more. I am getting help writing this letter, because my English isn't as good as I thought when I studied it in Havana. People here speak so quickly, and often I can't understand them.

We need to hear our parents' voices but haven't received a call. Could you please help us call them by telephone? I know they must be trying to call, but there are so many children in our camp that they probably are having a hard time reaching us. My brother and I must stay together when your organization finds a temporary home for us. I pray that you and God will make this happen. My brother is too little to be without me.

Please tell me why we are called "Pedro Pan" children. The nuns and priests have explained it differently. We heard that a boy named Pedro came to you when you decided to help bring the Cuban children over to Miami. You helped him, and then gave the program his name. We also heard that "pan," the Spanish word for "bread," is what he asked from you.

Father Menendez told my brother and his friends that there is an English story about lost children and an older boy named Peter Pan, who took them to his magical Neverland. I think their parents found them after a while, and they all went back home. We cannot go back home but we can wait for our parents to come to us. He told the boys that we are now like the lost children, at least until our parents come to America to find us. I think I like this story better and I hope it's the true reason we are called Pedro Pans.

I wish we had relatives in Miami so we could go live with them. I also want to write to President and Mrs. Kennedy, like some others from my camp have already done. I pray he might help us get our parents here faster. But Mr. George told me to write to you first, and I believe he knows what is best.

Thank you for allowing us to continue with our Catholic Mass and our religion classes. Thank you for letting the Cuban priests and nuns teach us, and for also allowing us to speak Spanish during our meals

and play time. I think that makes us feel a little better.
Thank you for being a very good man.

Sincerely yours,
Liliana Escobár

"What a beautiful letter, George." Tears were forming in Father Walsh's eyes as he closed the envelope. "I would like to meet her and answer all her questions."

"You could," George exclaimed. "The priests and the nuns of Camp Kendall have decided to have a Mother's Day celebration next week. Why don't you attend?"

Father Walsh cocked his head, with a quizzical expression. "What could I do at that event?"

"You could warm the hearts of all the children separated from their mothers," he replied firmly. "Just think of the joy you could bring them with your kind words." George smiled broadly.

Father Walsh hesitated. "Let me consider it, George. I do like your idea. I might be able to lift up their spirits."

"But in the meantime, I want to see what I can do for the Escobár children. We must keep them together, especially after reading that heartfelt plea from young Liliana."

After George left the office, Father Walsh re-read her letter. He was pleased by her interest in continuing religious classes. He and James Baker had insisted that the children maintain their religious upbringing, both in the camps and also in the foster homes. As far as he knew, this was being done.

He decided to make a phone call. He wanted this Mother's Day celebration at Kendall to be a success, if only for the children who were all separated from their mothers. He believed Katherine Brownell Oettinger, Chief of the

Children's Bureau, would provide the funding and more importantly, get some enthusiastic helpers with fresh ideas to make this a happy occasion.

"Oh Father Walsh, I think that's a marvelous idea," agreed Katherine, after listening to his suggestion. "And I know that Mrs. Oteisa, a former teacher at the Ruston Academy in Havana, will know exactly what to do. Let me contact her and get back to you."

"Thank you so much, Katherine. The Lord has answered this latest need through you and your willingness to help. I am well pleased," he said contentedly.

After hanging up, Father Walsh began writing down his responses to the young child who needed his support. Then he checked his calendar for a time to meet with her and her brother. Hopefully, he could give them advice and hope.

"Let Your will be done, my Lord," he implored. "I am simply Your humble servant."

7

May 6, 1961

Because calling Cuba from the United States was so difficult—sometimes taking twenty-four hours to place a call—we were told to write our parents letters first. We all wanted to share our honest feelings but were encouraged by the nuns to avoid writing any negative "words that might hurt." Sometimes they even asked us if they could read our letters before mailing them. I realized they were right and even helped Diego write comforting words.

We described our adjustment problems and possible solutions, our new friends and our studies, and said how much we missed them. Usually, I would start the letter and Diego would write something similar at the bottom of the page.

Before my best camp friend Estela left to meet her foster family, she gave me another piece of good advice. "Liliana, I know my parents need to believe that we are fine and happy, so that's what I write them. They can't help us with our situation here, and by not complaining about things, we are sparing them sadness."

I understood her point and tried to follow her example. We'd been here only three weeks, yet I found myself sharing more of my true feelings than perhaps I should have.

Dear Mami and Papi,

Diego and I are fine, and keep busy learning new things. It will be Mother's Day soon, and the nuns and priests are going to give us a sort of celebration, which will probably make us miss you even more. I know there will be new games and special foods and ice cream, which makes Diego very happy. He still cannot adjust to the food here and always brags about your cooking, Mami.

We want you to come soon, because if not, we will probably be sent to a foster family, maybe even far from Miami. Then it will be more difficult for you to find us when you come. And the weather might be cold in the wintertime, which I don't think you will like.

We both are enjoying our new friends and the school studies. Our English has improved, but we are allowed to speak Spanish to each other and the others when we aren't in classes. We also occasionally watch an American television program on the weekend to help us understand "slang," which we could call "modismos."

I am helping Diego feel more adjusted, and sometimes he helps me. Today I cried in Chapel after praying the Rosary. Then I asked God to make it easier to survive this time away from you, and I knew that He will always answer my prayers.

We really need to hear your voices on the telephone and also to receive another letter. We share the only one we have, and also my autograph book. One of us keeps the letter for a few days, and the other has the autograph book by our bed. Then we switch off, which makes us feel so much closer to you.

Please continue writing us about our friends and

give us some news of home. Also, tell us how you are working hard to come join us here. We miss you terribly but will stay strong.

Your two children who love you very much,
Liliana and Diego

P.S. This is Diego. I am fine. The food here is awful. But the candies are good. I have many friends now, and I see Lili almost every day. I miss you and hope you can phone us soon. I miss your voices. I love you so much.

One evening I was eating supper when Sister Josefina suddenly dashed into the dining room. "Liliana, come quickly! Your parents are on the phone!"

"Oh my goodness! Josefina, Diego's in his own camp eating supper, but please run and get him! He will be so excited!" I called out to her. My chair went flying as I raced to the visitor's room and the telephone.

"¡Mami! Papi! ¿Son ustedes de verdad? (Is it really you)?"

"We are here, querida Liliana. We finally got the phone call through." I could hear the tears in my mother's trembling voice.

"Where is Diego?" asked my father. Then his voiced softened. "Oh, how good it is to hear your voice, Lili."

"He's coming right away, Papi. He's in his own camp eating supper, but someone has gone to get him." My heart was lodged in my throat. "I cannot believe I am finally hearing you. How we've missed your voices," I stammered, fighting back a new wave of tears.

Fortunately, just then Diego ran into the room and grabbed the phone from me. "Mami, Papi, los quiero mucho. (I love you so much). When are you coming for us?"

"Oh Diego, we are trying so hard to get the visas. It won't be long now," our father told us.

"We only have one letter from you. Have you written more?" I was sure they had been writing a lot.

"Oh yes, my loves," responded Mami. "We write you several letters a week. I hope more will reach you soon, but the mail in and out of Cuba is not secure anymore. The regime reads all the letters and often doesn't deliver them."

"Papi, how long have you waited to get the call to us?" asked Diego, always curious about the details.

"We've been waiting about two hours to get through, but it's worth every second to finally hear your voices," he assured us warmly.

"Tell us that you are well, happy and studying hard," Papi commanded, in his strict but loving style.

"Yes, Papi. We are doing well, but we won't be happy until you are with us again." I shot a stern look at Diego, hoping he would not disagree or make it a joke. He didn't.

Then we heard two clicks, and the connection was broken. I put my hand over my mouth to cover up my sob. Diego reached over and touched my hand to comfort me.

I was touched. "Thank you, *hermanito* (little brother). This has become the best day we've had in Miami, hasn't it?"

He smiled. "And we just wrote them another letter, so that's worth a double payout, right?"

I scowled. "Diego, what do you know about payouts? Are you gambling over there in your camp?"

"Just for desserts, Lil. You know we don't have money, and the coins I do have I'm saving for treats over the weekend."

"Let me tell you a secret, Diego," I grinned. "I think we might be meeting Father Walsh at the Mother's Day celebration. I overheard one of the nuns saying he wants to come, and so we can meet him then. Now that's what I call a *double payout.*"

He was suddenly serious, and something shifted in his eyes. "Sis, I really miss Mami and Papi. When I hear their voices, it makes me feel worse."

"That's only for a second, Diego. Hold the precious memories close to your heart, and they'll keep us strong until we see them again."

We returned to our suppers, happy to have special news to share with our new friends.

8

Mother's Day May 14, 1961

We were very excited the Sunday morning of Mother's Day. They told us this was the first Mother's Day celebration at Camp Kendall. Father Menendez said we would be honoring our mothers for allowing us to leave Cuba to save us from communist indoctrination and economic hardship. The priests and nuns and other camp employees had pooled their money to buy every one of us a red carnation, as a tribute to our mothers.

We crafted Mother's Day cards with their names hand-painted on the top, over a special poem that we really liked or had written ourselves. I chose one that said exactly what I felt, and then designed red tissue paper carnations to paste alongside the words.

> *Todos tienen una madre*
> *Y yo tengo la mejor.*
> *La que me llena de besos*
> *De esperanzas y de amor.*
> (Everyone has a mother
> And I have the best.
> One who fills me up with kisses
> Of hopes and of love).

Diego wanted to write his own poem to her, and I think he did a very nice job.

> *Mi Mami no está aquí conmigo*
> *Pero está en mi corazón.*
> *Sabe que la quiero*
> *Y me extraña todos los días y noches,*
> *Como yo la extraño también.*
> (My mother isn't here with me
> But she's in my heart.
> She knows I love her
> And she misses me every day and night,
> Just like I miss her).

We got help with the translations, so everyone could save their cards and present them to our mothers when we finally see them again. The older girls helped the younger girls and boys create decorative tissue paper flowers. All of the colorful craft materials had been donated by people who wanted to support Pedro Pan children.

The adults strung the cards on clotheslines stretched between dining area walls. This was our first "all camp" party and we felt the energy filling the room. Arm in arm, we girls walked around reading and admiring everyone's art. Some of boys followed us; others played in the patio.

After a while, we were summoned to come to the tables to enjoy Sunday lunch together.

After lunch, we learned that the cooks in both camps had been very busy secretly baking chocolate, banana, white and marble cakes, and even lemon tortes. They were so tasty and we even got second helpings, to the delight of Diego and his friends. We listened to Cuban and American music on records while we ate dessert; then the door opened and three men walked into the dining room.

"Oh my, it's Father Walsh!" whispered my friend Maria. "He's with George and another man. I wonder who that is."

Most of us knew George, since he'd picked us up from the airport and had visited the camp a few times. Many of the others knew Father Walsh, but only those who had attended his school in Havana recognized James Baker. He was the director of the Ruston Academy, and one of the first people to help get children out of Cuba.

On stage, they were greeted by Father Menendez and several Cuban nuns.

"May I have your attention, please?" Father Menendez turned on the microphone. A huge smile spread across his face.

"I am so proud and happy to introduce Father Walsh and James Baker to you. I know you've all met Jorge Guarch, who you know as 'George,' and some of you might also know James Baker. He and Father Walsh are the reason you all are here. Without their constant work and backing, the visa program would never have happened, including the tickets purchased to fly you here. Please give them the thanks that they deserve."

We looked at each other and began to clap politely. The men smiled, and then Father Walsh was handed the microphone.

"I am Father Walsh, and I am so happy that we could join you today in honoring your mothers. This is our first Mothers' Day Celebration at Camp Kendall. You all know, better than I, that your mothers have done their very best to care for you, educate you and protect you. Along with your fathers, they all made the ultimate sacrifice: to give up their children temporarily to provide you a safer life and freedom."

Total silence followed as we digested everything he was saying.

Clearing his throat, he continued. "Today could be a very sad day for you, separated and far away from your mothers and fathers. But we, and all of the employees here, have committed our resources and our work to getting you reunited with them. So let us make this a day of joy and gratitude."

His humble smile seemed to glow as he finished. This time the applause was resounding. George quietly left the stage and walked up to me. He whispered that Father Walsh would like to meet me and my brother in the visitors' room in about five minutes. I looked at Diego and gave him the great news. I was so excited!

We rose and began to move from the table. Several children crowded the stage, wanting to speak to the guests. I asked Josefina to bring Diego back inside, since he had already rushed outside to play. Then we walked into the visitors' room to meet with Father Walsh.

9

May 14, 1961

We didn't have long to wait. Diego and I sat on a sofa, our red carnations in hand, when Father Walsh entered the room. I nudged my brother and whispered, "Stand up."

Father Walsh smiled broadly and extended his hand. We each shook it, then returned to the sofa as he settled in a high-backed wing chair.

"I've been waiting for this happy day for a while now," he told us. "Especially to have the opportunity to meet both of you."

"Thank you, Father Walsh," I managed to say, suddenly overcome with shyness.

"Liliana, you wrote me a beautiful letter, and I'm happy to answer your questions now." Turning to Diego, he continued. "Diego, I have heard good reports about you and how well you help the new boys get settled in."

Diego squirmed in his chair, unprepared for Father Walsh's praise. I smiled gently, hoping to put him at ease.

"It just so happens that I also have some good news to share with you both, which I believe will make you happy." He leaned forward in his chair and reached into his pouch for a piece of paper.

"But first, I understand that just recently you spoke with your parents. Is this true?"

"Oh yes, Father," Diego exclaimed. "And they are doing everything to come here with us!"

He nodded, studying our faces. Then he turned to me with an expression of quiet strength and serenity.

"Liliana, regarding your letter, I fully agree that you and Diego must stay together. It's taken a little longer to find a family who can take you both, but we are persistent." His voice softened, "You thanked me for our Kendall Camp policy of following the religious training the children received in Cuba. I am so happy we've been able to provide that for you and Diego."

Father Walsh paused, and the corners of his eyes crinkled. "I've also heard excellent reports on how well you encourage and help the others here, both the girls and the boys."

We sat quietly, wondering where the conversation was heading.

"Liliana, you asked me about *Operation Pedro Pan*, which you now know is the name of the program that brought you and the others here." His expression became thoughtful.

"In November of 1960 a fifteen-year-old lad named Pedro Menendez came to me for help, and we gave him food and shelter. He was the first, but it quickly escalated once Mr. Baker and I began to fly the first children out of Havana to Miami. The first flight was on December 26th of last year. A Christmas gift that many of us celebrated."

"President Eisenhower gave us one million dollars from his administration to fund this program. We will keep soliciting donations from other organizations, for as long as this program continues," he promised proudly.

After a few moments, I asked him. "How many of us have you brought over so far?"

"Almost a thousand have arrived, and we are quickly running out of temporary shelters here in Miami."

"And how many have been reunited with their parents?"

"We have kept records, but not enough time has passed to get many reunited yet." "However," he added confidently, "we have received more and more visas for the parents in these past few weeks."

A smile spread across his face. "Now, let's move on to your good news."

He cleared his throat. "We have found a couple in Oregon who wants to be your foster family until your parents arrive. They and their two children, about the same ages as you, are happy to welcome both of you."

Diego spoke first. "Where is Oregon? Is it cold there?"

Father Walsh laughed. "It's on the other side of the country Diego, on the west coast. And yes, in the winter it can be cold."

"Will there be snow?" he pressed on.

"I think so, but for half the year it will be warm, just like here . . . except without the humidity."

I listened to their conversation, my mind bubbling with questions. I was stunned. My whole body felt hot. That was so far away from Cuba.

Father Walsh noticed. "Liliana, is something wrong? You look flushed."

I stared at him blankly. "When would we leave? Is there time to discuss this with our parents?"

He stood up and walked slowly toward the sofa. Taking both of my hands in his, he said gently, "I think it will take about two weeks before you could go, and I'll make sure your parents have all the details and give us their approval," he assured me with a compassionate smile.

Diego looked unsettled.

Father Walsh softened his voice. "Let me get more details and we can speak again about this opportunity. I want you both to be in agreement before we accept this offer."

We nodded, and he turned to leave. First he paused to bless us, placing his warm hand on our heads. "Thank you again for all you do for the children here."

I answered a bit awkwardly. "Thank you, Father Walsh, for all you do for the Pedro Pans. And thank you for answering my letter in person and offering us this new possibility." I fought back tears as he walked toward the door.

"Bye, Father Walsh," Diego called out, following him out. Then he turned around to see how I was feeling.

"I'm fine," I reassured him. "I just want to go lay down in my room for a little while."

He nodded, handing me his red carnation and Mother's Day card for safekeeping.

10

May 25, 1961

It was settled. The next day we would fly to Beaverton, Oregon, where the Rustin family would become our foster family until our parents could pick us up.

Father Walsh contacted Mami and Papi by telegram, and they gave *Operation Pedro Pan* permission to send us to Oregon. We would fly from Miami to Chicago, then from Chicago to Portland, Oregon.

He told us our parents had sounded pleased to learn that we'd be living with two other children our ages.

"The weather will be warm, and the summer trees and flowers are in bloom," he said. "You will be very comfortable in Beaverton."

In the month that we'd been here at the camp, I had already said goodbye to a few friends who had moved on. I even heard back from two of them. Estela wrote that she had a very good *beca*, meaning that she was happy with her foster parents and even liked her school. In the beginning, we had thought *beca* meant the scholarship we'd receive, but by now we knew it was really our "future placement."

One of the nuns gave us a quick geography lesson on Oregon. She showed us a few photos of Beaverton, the small town close to Portland where we would be living. And yesterday, Mr. and Mrs. Rustin even phoned us to let us know they would be waiting at the airport tomorrow afternoon. They also said they were very excited that we were coming to live with them.

Both Diego and I felt good about our *beca*, and silently prayed that it would be a fine transition. Two more letters had arrived from our parents, just two days apart. They promised they would try to phone us soon after our arrival in Oregon. They said they missed hearing our voices.

Earlier this afternoon Diego asked me why we would have to go to school in Oregon.

"Diego, we need to keep learning English, and also the other subjects everyone needs to know," I answered.

"Like what?" He was not happy about one more change in schools.

"Like what we have been studying here, and back in Cuba. History, mathematics, literature. You know, *hermanito.*"

He nodded solemnly. "Father Menendez says that when we go back to Cuba we'll be educated and can help shape the future of our country."

"When Cuba becomes free, we'll do just that," I agreed, surprised at Father Menendez's comment.

After dinner, we returned to our bunks to pack our few possessions. I sat and re-read some of the many entries in my diary, which was really my autograph book. Then I placed it on the bottom of my duffel bag.

Then I picked up Olguita and held her to my heart. "Thank you *querida* (dear one)." I knew I wouldn't need her help anymore. Carrying her lovingly to sweet six-year-old Mireya, who cried herself to sleep every night, I saw the wonder in her eyes when I gave her my doll.

"*¿Para mi?* (For me)? *¿Para siempre?* (For always)?" Her eyes sparkled with pleasure.

I smiled and hugged her. "*Tú la necesitas más que yo. Cuidála bien. Ya eres su mamita.* (You need her more than I do. Take good care of her. Now you are her mama)."

May 26, 1961

Our flight on Delta Airlines left at nine o'clock in the morning. George picked us up and stayed with us until we walked to the boarding gate. When we said good-bye to him, he handed us an envelope.

"Be safe, be blessed, and be happy," he grinned. "Father Walsh wanted you to have this so you'll also be a little independent."

"Open it, Lil. Let's see what we have!" Diego burst out.

"Let's wait until we are in our seats and the plane is off the ground," I suggested. He stuck out his lip in a pout, but agreed.

"Señor George, we will miss you. Thank you for making this past month easier than it would have been without you," I said. After a warm hug, I added, "May God always protect you."

"I will write you," Diego assured him. George grinned and nodded.

It was much easier settling into our seats for this flight than the one just a month ago. No one was crying, we were going to join another "family," and we were together. I believed we were also one step closer to seeing our parents. I whispered a small prayer of gratitude.

"Lil, let's open the card now," Diego persisted. I laughed and got it from my purse.

Inside the envelope were two ten dollar bills and a kind note from *Operation Pedro Pan*. Once again I felt tears burning behind my eyes.

Diego brought me back to reality. "Oh my goodness, Liliana. Look at this! We're rich!" He beamed with pleasure.

I hugged him fiercely. "Yes we are, and in so many ways." Diego struggled when I put my hands on his cheeks to kiss him.

"Now, can we rest? We have a long day ahead of us." I closed my eyes, and in less than a minute was sound asleep. When I woke up, it was time for lunch.

11

May 26, 1961

Our foster family was waiting for us near the exit, waving and holding up a sign: *Welcome to Oregon, Diego and Liliana.*

We just stood there, clutching our duffel bags and watching them approach us, wearing big friendly smiles. I stuck out my hand as Mr. Rustin reached me, but instead of shaking it, he leaned over and wrapped me in a hug. It felt so good.

Mrs. Rustin also embraced us. The children said hello and looked us over. Their names are Annette and Sebastian. Annette is fourteen, and Sebastian is nine.

Annette is very pretty. Our eyes are almost the same color: blue-green like the ocean. She has very blond hair (mine is dark blonde with streaks of honey). Diego and Sebastian have dark brown hair, but Diego's eyes are big, brown and round; Sebastian's are a vivid blue. I would often be surprised at how well we got along, beginning with that very first meeting. Another blessing!

We drove about a half an hour to Beaverton. I realized we could actually carry on a conversation with them, even though our English was still poor. Only once did I have to ask Mrs. Rustin to speak a little more slowly so I could understand everything.

She grinned. "Of course, dear. I am so excited that you're here that I seem to be rambling."

Diego looked confused. "What is rambling?" he wanted to know.

Mr. Rustin's jovial burst of laughter could be heard throughout the car. He looked through his rear view mirror and noticed Diego's surprised expression. "I'm not laughing at you, son. I'm laughing because that's the word I use with my wife when she goes on and on about something."

Diego frowned, looking more confused. Mrs. Rustin sent him a sweet smile. "What 'ramble' means, Diego, is 'wandering off the point' while talking. Sometimes I go totally off topic, but I'll try not to ramble until you and Liliana understand our American slang."

When I had the opportunity, I whispered the translation to Diego in Spanish. He said to them, "Oh, yes. My sister Liliana does that too. My mom also." Now we all laughed together. This was a great introduction for us.

Mrs. Rustin spoke slowly as we drove up to the garage. "Our home is a ranch style, which you may not have seen in Havana. It's a one level house with large living areas. I'll show you around once we drop off your bags in your rooms."

Annette explained excitedly, "Liliana and I will share my room, and you boys will be in Sebastian's room." I smiled, glancing at Diego, who seemed pleased with the news.

"Oh my," I exclaimed, as we entered the house. "This is such a lovely home. Look at all the large windows and the wooden floors." I glanced up at the ceiling. "And the ceiling is so high."

Mr. and Mrs. Rustin grinned at our wide-eyed reactions. "Let's take them to their rooms, dear," suggested Mr. Rustin.

I felt like we had been transported to a magical place, compared to the cramped quarters in our camp dormitories. Annette's bedroom was beautiful, decorated in a tangerine color that reminded me of Havana's sunsets. I had to force myself not to get emotional, so I spoke up. "This is so pretty, and thank you for sharing it with me, Annette. We were very crowded in our bunk rooms at the camp in Miami." I looked around in wonder. "I cannot believe we each have a large bed here, and our very own dresser." I was not prepared for such generous accommodations.

"Let's go to our room," prompted Diego. Sebastian grinned and led him to the next room.

"Wow! This is so good," he blurted out in Spanish. "Lili, come over here and look at all the toys and planes and games they have!" Diego's eyes were sparkling with pleasure. I had not seen him this interested in anything since we left Cuba. I felt my eyes filling with tears, and quickly swiped at them.

"Well, I'm going to get dinner started. Annette and Sebastian, why don't you take Liliana and Diego down to the basement and then show them the back yard," suggested Mrs. Rustin. I think she understood my emotional state. "Oh, and let them try out their bicycles."

"Bicycles? We have our own bicycles?" Now I was the one who was shocked.

"The kids thought you'd like to ride with them through the neighborhood and out on the trails, so we got them as your welcome gift. Go have a look." Mr. Rustin smiled.

We spent the next hour exploring the back yard and riding our bicycles around the neighborhood. When we came in for dinner, I wandered through all the rooms, admiring the brick fireplace, the daylight basement, which they called a walk out, and led right to the back yard. They had three bathrooms in the house and very pretty woodwork. My Papi would love the floors and the woodwork, since he also likes to carve.

During dinner, Mr. Rustin asked us about our home in Cuba.

"We have a beautiful home in Havana, but it is very different," I began. "Our home is typical Cuban middle of the century style, painted a colorful canary yellow. The main house is divided into smaller apartments: two on each floor, and another at the back of the patio, created from the garage."

Diego joined in. "And we have a patio with many fruit trees like mameys, mangos, limes and a lot of palm trees."

"That must be so lovely, and it sounds like it gives you privacy," said Mrs. Rustin.

"Yes, it does, especially on the patio, where we also have a pool. Many of the older homes do," I added. "But here, I love seeing open neighborhoods, with the woods just two blocks away."

"Are your floors made of marble?" Mr. Rustin seemed very interested in the materials.

"Yes," answered Diego. "Isn't that marble on our floors, Lil?"

I nodded. "And our second floor is reached by a double staircase in the living room. That's where our bedrooms are." Suddenly, I felt nostalgic for my home and my family in a wave of emotion. The scent of jasmine accompanied a memory of our Cuban gardens.

I offered to help clean up after the meal, but Mrs. Rustin insisted that she and Annette would do that today.

I felt very weary and fatigued. I wanted to be alone and go to sleep. I think Annette picked up on that.

"Why don't you go shower in our bathroom and get

ready for bed," she suggested. "I know you are very tired from your long flight. I'll join you later."

I nodded in relief and followed her advice. I knew we were so much better off here than at our camp, but I didn't want to think about my friends there, or my family in Cuba. I felt so far away from everything that is familiar to us. And now that I didn't have my doll Olguita, I even missed her. Smiling, I remembered Mireya's happy face when she first hugged the doll.

After my shower, I went to wish everyone a good night. The parents were in the living room, watching television. Annette was in the kitchen, reading a school book. The boys were nowhere to be seen.

"Annette, do you know where the boys are?"

She smiled. "Outside, riding their bicycles. But they have to be back here just before dark. Sebastian knows."

I smiled a tired smile. "Please wish my brother a good night for me. And you too. I'll see you in the morning." To my great surprise, she stepped forward to hug me. There was emotion and kindness in the hug. I hugged her back.

I feel asleep in thankful prayer, sending my parents loving thoughts.

12

June 15, 1961

I woke up suddenly, heart pounding. The dream was vivid and real. I could see myself sitting on the bed, my mother's arms locked around me. Then, I lifted up and I felt myself floating, drifting above everything but not quite flying. I looked down at my mother weeping, and then over at my father for confirmation. I found it there, in his glistening eyes. "Fly, fly away," he whispered. He was trying to tell me more, but no more words were audible. My mother's face appeared much older, sadness pulling at all her features. I watched my body slowly float away.

Bolting upright, I gulped in as much oxygen as I could, and then blew it out slowly. This was the worst nightmare yet, but at least I understood that it wasn't my real life. Shaking my head helped to clear it.

At this early morning hour, I decided to write an updated message of all the good things that have happened to us since we came to Oregon. Already some nice things have become a part of our new lives, and I vaguely wondered if I'd written about them in my diary. Both Diego and I were grateful for our blessings. So why did I still have nightmares?

I tiptoed out of the room and went to the kitchen. Turning on the light, I began to write.

1. Our parents phoned us two days after we got to Oregon, and we spoke with them for about 15 minutes. Everyone cried, including Diego, but we ended up laughing together and promising to write more often.

2. We started school right after we arrived, and even though our English is not up to our age level, most people understand us and tell us they like our "accents."

3. I have made some friends in the seventh grade and I especially like my teacher, Mrs. Bailey. She compliments me all the time and makes me want to work harder to please her.

4. We all went shopping for clothes, and the kids helped Diego and me pick out styles that are popular here. It's getting warmer so our Cuban outfits are fine, but definitely more elegant than what they wear in Oregon. And we certainly needed more than what we had brought. The Rustins wouldn't let us use our own money that Operation Pedro Pan had given us, so we're able to save that. And, since we help out with household chores (something we never did in Cuba because we had maids), we get an allowance and have been able to add more to our original ten dollars. I think we'll be using some of it during summer break, because we'll have a lot of free time and I think we're going to travel somewhere. Also, we're both saving most of our money to send to our parents for their airplane tickets.

5. Diego also likes second grade and is happy he and Sebastian are in the same school. This makes Diego feel

*comfortable because they can sit together on the bus. I
ride with my new friends on a different bus.*

6. *Annette has been a great "big sister" to us. She goes to
another school and Mr. Rustin usually takes her, but
sometimes she rides with a friend's parents. We all
have breakfast together every morning, even though
it's much earlier than when we had breakfast in Cuba.
School starts earlier too, and finishes earlier. So we have
lots of free time before we have to do chores or homework.*

7. *American breakfasts are very different from ours. They
love cereal, both hot and cold, and nobody (except the
adults) drinks coffee. Eggs and bacon are only served on
weekends, and they eat toasted bread instead of the sweet
breads we had in Havana. I still like Cuban breakfasts
better. Oh, and I also like Cuban dinners better. I miss
the way Cubans cook black and red beans, rice and pica-
dillo, and I also miss Cuban bread. But Mrs. Rustin has
made us some good American meals too.*

8. *The Rustins are also Catholic, and we always attend
Mass together. I smile as I remember that Father Walsh
told me they try to send children to families of the same
faith. I am beginning to learn more about our religion
through classes that we go to twice a month. Both Diego
and I like them. And hearing Mass in Latin takes me
back to the days and the church in Cuba, with my family sitting together. Somehow, that helps me deal with
my homesickness.*

9. *We don't have as much homework as we did in Havana. Our schools here are public, not private like there, and our teachers are not nuns or priests. I think if I had perfect English I would get perfect grades, but I'm not doing badly. Diego struggles more than I do, but he doesn't care. His sense of humor gets him through and has made him lots of friends.*

10. *Yes, I still do miss Cuba: my parents, my friends, my grandparents, my school, my home. I hope that soon my parents will be here, and we'll all be together. I don't know where we'll live, or what work my father will do (he's a pharmacist in Havana and I have heard that he will have to study that degree again here to do the same work) but I just feel sure that we'll be fine.*

11. *I am happy that I am almost bilingual. I think I will always have a Latin accent, which is good, because I am proud to be a Cuban. I am so pleased to be doing well in this country and, like other Cuban Pedro Pans I know, to have such a good "beca" with the Rustin family.*

12. *Diego and I have written to "Operation Pedro Pan," thanking Father Walsh, George and James Baker for all they have done for us. We also wrote to our friends, the nuns and the priests at Camp Kendall. Mami would be so happy to know that we remembered the manners she taught us.*

13. *In just two weeks, school will be out for summer vacation. We have some plans for travel—I'm not supposed to know this but I heard we're going to Disneyland! Mr. and Mrs. Rustin asked us what we wanted for our "end*

of the school" gift. Diego and I decided that we'd love to be able to call Mami and Papi in Cuba. We promised to only speak fifteen minutes because we know how expensive it is, but they said we could talk as long as we wanted to. They are so good to us.

14. *I am grateful for this beautiful place to live, where we are almost happy. Some days I don't even remember how much I want to see my parents, and here in Oregon letters arrive more frequently than when we lived in Miami. I try to remember to thank God every night for our blessings.*

After writing that long list, I folded it and put it in my drawer. I will take it to school and make a copy to send to my family in Cuba. I know they will enjoy it, and I'll also include some news about what we did the past week. Papi tells me reading our weekly letters is the best part of his week, and I believe him. Mr. Rustin has taken some Polaroid camera pictures that I will include and hope the soldiers censuring the mail will not remove them.

We've heard almost nothing about Castro or Cuba here on the news and the Rustins say that Cuban news is not in the local newspapers. Sometimes an American friend mentions something their parents saw in a magazine, but so far, we haven't seen anything. I've received two letters from girlfriends still in Cuba, saying it's even worse than when we left. They can't specify because then the letters would be destroyed, so I have to ask Mami and Papi guarded questions when we speak on the phone, and they can't give us details. I will write to Father Walsh and ask him to be honest with me. But for now, I'm sleepy and still have time to sleep a few more hours.

13

July 15, 1961

Seven people were gathered in Father Walsh's small office to discuss Camp Matecumbe, the newest location they found to house teenage boys from twelve to fifteen years old.

"We need to move them from Camp Kendall and several other places," he was explaining. "I know the location is not perfect, since it is south of Miami, but we'll have the room to house and school at least three hundred fifty teenagers."

"Will we have the staff for the facility?" wondered James Baker. Others nodded, concerned with this unexpected news.

"The Brothers of La Salle will run it, and will bring in several priests from other orders. We're also looking at Florida City, but that is thirty-five miles south of Miami near Homestead. Girls will have to be placed there as well."

A staffer who helped oversee the expenses groaned aloud.

Father Walsh continued. "Our mission is to help every child, recently separated from families, to begin a new life in safe, caring and supportive environments. As the numbers grow precipitously, our ability to make sure they are in perfect families will get harder. Also, once they're placed with foster families, we must accept responsibility for handling any relationship problem quickly. Otherwise, that burden falls on the child's shoulders . . . and they simply don't have the maturity, experience and resources to take care of themselves in unfamiliar situations."

"We've got to get more financial backing to care adequately for so many children," commented the staffer. Several others nodded in agreement.

Father Walsh raised his hand for quiet. "Please stay calm. We will soon receive the second half of the four million dollars for the relief agencies—the aid that President Kennedy ordered in January."

"But the influx is already well over what we expected at this time. What can we do?"

Father Walsh appraised each of them in turn. "We will practice patience, and remember that He has guided us through all of this and even removed obstacles. He will continue to direct us now." His voice was soft, and a smile darted briefly across his face.

"Some of you have heard our *Operation Pedro Pan* being compared to the *Kindertransport*. Just prior to the outbreak of World War II, that rescue mission saved more than ten thousand children from the Holocaust."

Many nodded, recognizing the comparison.

After a thoughtful silence, Father Edwards spoke. "Father Walsh, may I change the subject for a moment?"

"Yes, Father Edwards. What is on your mind?"

"Thank you. Going back to Matecumbe, wasn't that recently a summer retreat for priests? If so, it should be in very good condition, am I correct?"

"Yes, it has everything we need for the boys. It was also a summer camp for Catholic youth, and the facilities are adequate for beds, meals and school rooms."

Another priest voiced his concern. "I fear the number

of children exiting Cuba will overwhelm our capacities. Especially now that you, Father Walsh, are in a position to issue visa waivers for the children under eighteen."

"But remember, Father Villanueva, there is a caveat. Those teenagers between the ages of sixteen and eighteen have to pass a security clearance to leave Cuba. And that will include many in the underground network—those very children whose parents would suffer repercussions if caught."

Father Villanueva raised his eyebrows and shrugged slightly. "I understand now. Is that also why *Operation Pedro Pan* has become classified in the U.S.?"

"Indeed it is. Now we can house those same children openly. The Castro regime will never know where those who leave the country have resettled."

Father Walsh stretched his legs and leaned back in his chair. "And this parallel program for the underground children has been expanded. We will be able to issue thousands of visa waivers to parents and children in the near future. That will reunite families much more quickly than even we imagined."

"Yes, Father. And I realize that it was because of the parents' concerns about their children and the reality that new rumors of *Patria Potestad* have emerged, which led to the mass exodus of the Pedro Pans."

"Forgive my ignorance, but I do not understand this *Patria Potestad*." Father Edwards had joined the *Operation Pedro Pan* office just a few weeks earlier.

"Yes, that is understandable." Father Walsh appreciated his honesty and liked his enthusiasm.

"After closing the schools in Cuba, Fidel Castro started a comprehensive education reform and sent over one thousand students to Russia. He then opened military post schools that many called 'indoctrination centers.' His plan was and still is to send these students into the countryside to teach the *campesinos* (peasants) how to read and more importantly, *what* to read."

He paused and cleared his throat. "Shortly after that reform, we began hearing rumors about *Patria Potestad*— the government's intention to take custody of children away from their parents, and remove the children from their homes to be educated under the Revolution's design. It would be a powerful form of *brainwashing* and made every family fearful for their children."

"Is this happening now?"

"We believe so, but more slowly than they hoped. It's the main reason for our thousands of requests for visas, by parents who fear what will happen to their children's minds. They consider education the determining factor for the destiny of the nation." Father Walsh finished bleakly.

James Baker had remained quiet during this exchange. Now he spoke up. "Let's talk a little about Polita Grau and her brother Mongo. As members of Cuba's political aristocracy, they have an extensive network of friends on the island, including many in the diplomatic corps. Without their interest, we would never have been able to bring over so many Cubans; and they still have a stronghold in the underground movement."

"And Penny Powers from the British Embassy will be their liaison with the Church. Mongo has agreed to distribute the visa waivers you sign, Father Walsh, and distribute the money orders for parents to buy seats for their children to fly to Miami." Although weary, Father Walsh's eyes shone with excitement as the discussion turned to his friends.

James Baker joined the conversation. "The travel agencies and the airlines, Pan Am and KLM, will hold seats for the children by wait-listing false names. And soon, we will be able to give Mongo the authority to issue visas to those under the age of sixteen," he added, grinning. "Just as Father Walsh has told you, the good Lord is carrying these movements on His wings."

"Are there any more questions?"

"Yes, Father Walsh. I have another one about a rumor I heard somewhere." The priest who spoke up had rarely spoken. "The woman's network, *Rescate de la Niñez*, (Rescue the Children) is also directed by Polita, isn't it?"

Father Walsh had hoped this wouldn't come up. His voice was almost a whisper. "Yes, it is."

"Did they provide the CIA with information on the Soviet missiles? Was this group involved in spying?"

Father Walsh hesitated so he could choose his words carefully. "Polita and her network were delegated the responsibility for the safe conduct of those fighting in the underground. When *Operation Pedro Pan* was started, she organized the entire women's group to help out, encouraging them to send their children out of Cuba and entrust their care to the Catholic Church."

"So the CIA was aware of her actions, correct?"

"I believe they were, Father Edwards. I know that Polita and her family used the Grau home in Havana, which was across the street from the Security Police offices, to establish their counterfeiting operation that issued out false passports through Panama's Embassy. Those with valid passports but outdated visas lined up to have the date changed by an artist working with Polita. And finally, those with valid passports but no visas had one stamped in with the official embassy stamp that was given to the Graus through their CIA contacts. The U.S. visas were valid for four years."

James Baker added. "Oh, and one last thing we should all be aware of: what these women did for *Patria Postestad*. *Rescate de la Niñez* became their battle cry: saving the children from the communist brainwashing was an extension to their commitment to protect the future for democracy.

"Both Father Walsh and I felt that because of the changing religious and political beliefs rising in Cuba, the children were better off away from their parents than in Cuba, where they would live with their families in an authoritarian state. We felt strongly that the children would be better served in a democratic country rather than under a communistic regime," explained James Baker."

"Is that how and why you began *Operation Pedro Pan*?" wondered Father Villanueva.

"Yes, it is. We hoped that democracy would eventually spread to Cuba, through these same children who would acquire a taste for it. With a little help from the United States of America," added James Baker proudly.

Father Walsh stood up, rubbing his tired eyes. "I think we've accomplished a great deal this afternoon and clarified the current situation. We'll be able to share new information next week. Thank you all for coming. Father Edwards, would you kindly close us in prayer?"

Then they headed out. It had been sprinkling only fifteen minutes earlier. Father Walsh reached for his umbrella, but then decided to leave it. Unexpected glimmers of brilliant sunshine were bursting through the black clouds, filling the somber sky with a beautiful radiance spreading from below the horizon. He caught his breath at the sudden beauty, and raising his eyes to the heavens, he smiled and crossed himself.

14

September 5, 1961

Today was our first day back to school after our long summer break. I still attend Beaverton Jr. High School, which serves grades seven and eight. I was a little nervous to board the bus because only a few of my friends are still riding it, but the day turned out well and I found my friends quickly.

Yesterday was Labor Day, which is a holiday here in America. I'm not sure what it's about, but it's a day off for most workers, although not for Mr. Rustin, because he is an attorney. The day after Labor Day is the first day of school, so we had enjoyed almost nine weeks of summer vacation. And it gave Diego and me a great opportunity to listen and learn the type of English they speak here, including the slang. We may always have our Latin accents, but everyone seems to like the way we speak, so we don't worry about it.

The Rustin family did take us to Disneyland! The car trip was long, but we spent the first night in a motel and also the final night before returning home. We had seen pictures and movies about Disneyland in Cuba, but discovered it is so much better when you are there! We were very lucky to have three entire days there, and we even stayed in the Disneyland Hotel! Diego said he's never spent a better three days in his life. He used his allowance to buy Mickey Mouse ears and other souvenirs. I only bought a picture book with great photos of the entire park. I know our parents will appreciate it.

Annette and Sebastian had been to the amusement park a few years after it opened, but still seemed as excited as we were to visit it again. I think we rode all the rides several times, saw all the shows, and spent hours riding around on the People Mover. My favorite ride was the Skyway, the gondola that took us from Tomorrowland to Fantasyland and back. It went through the Matterhorn Mountain, which was exciting. Diego's favorite ride was the Submarine Voyage. We all loved the Autopia, but Diego was too small to drive the cars so he had to ride with us. We could all board the Rocket Jets, which was Sebastian's favorite. And we enjoyed the food, especially the cotton candy.

My parents called us the day after we returned from that trip, and we shared our adventure stories with them. In that same conversation, Mami assured us that they would try to come here before the year ended. Papi didn't say anything when she talked about *when*, but he told us it would be "*lo más pronto possible* (before we knew it)." I hope and pray it will happen this year.

To be honest, I'm still just "almost" happy. I know I should be totally happy, because I have a good life here and the Rustins treat us like their own children. I feel like they really do care about us, and we've only been here for four months. Diego and I have become very attached to them. Annette and Sebastian are like our brother and sister. But . . . we still don't have our parents here to share this with.

I always believed I was a kind, unselfish girl. I think God wanted me to care more about other people and recognize their needs. The Bible teaches us to help each other and be aware of how our actions affect every life we touch. God gave me the kind of family and childhood experiences I'd need to follow His commands.

I really believe that Cubans can be some of the world's most caring and cooperative people. The Bible shapes the way we live and think and overcome hardships. So becoming a truly unselfish girl who thinks of other people first and then finds something positive in every situation isn't just about being a good Christian. My responsibility as a proud Cubana is to always be someone that others can look up to.

God brought us to the United States to be with people who have different lives but similar hearts. Whatever my future may bring, I want to be known as a Cubana who made many people's worlds brighter and more hopeful—like Father Walsh does.

Because that will make Mami and Papi proud.

The rest of the summer was full of surprises. We traveled to a small town on the Oregon Coast called Manzanita (*little apple* in Spanish). We stayed in a bungalow overlooking the cold Pacific Ocean. Having grown up in Havana, we had no idea the ocean could be this cold. Or such a dark, almost angry color. Where were the blues, the turquoises, the greens of the ocean in Cuba and Miami?

We really liked the foggy air and the huge mountains towering above us. I was amazed by their height and shapes. We opened the car door and smelled the sea and the sharp tang of rosemary and pine. Then we heard the slap of the waves hitting the rocky shore.

Diego and I laughed gleefully. We'd never seen a rocky beach. I tipped my head back to take in the sound: big and flowing. The fog was freakish, but not scary. It covered my face and didn't seem to lift up. It felt like the air had turned into a thick soup.

"How do you walk in this?" I asked Annette and Sebastian. "Can you swim here?"

She giggled. "Oh no, it's very cold. We walk the beach and enjoy the rocks and the sea animals."

"But it's summer," Diego informed her. "That's when it should be warm."

"Not on the Oregon coast," Sebastian confirmed. "But we'll take you on some great hikes, and you'll see why we like it so much."

A smile spread across Diego's face. "Let's go!" he commanded. And off they went.

I turned to Annette. "To think that my parents and I were so worried that Diego would not be able to adjust. He told me yesterday that he's praying I can survive the changes to come."

"That's pretty perceptive of him. What did you say?"

"I said, "I will, Diego, but I'll do much better when we can share it with Mami and Papi.""

Last week Annette found me sobbing on my bed. "Are you missing your parents?" she asked softly, kneeling on the carpet next to my bed.

I nodded. "It's so hard sometimes," I wept, wiping at my eyes.

She stroked my hair and let me cry.

"Lili, I truly believe in my heart that they will be here before the year is over. Perhaps in time for Christmas. Then we'll all celebrate it together." Her eyes smiled. "Just put your heart where your hope is."

Her words softened my despair. They sounded like something my Papi would have said. I hugged her.

"Want to go for a bike ride?" I asked.

"Race you to the woods!" she challenged.

"Let's go," I knew that nature, the sky and the birds were the best remedies to my sadness.

Yet three days later, it happened all over again. I was home alone catching up on my homework. Everyone else had someplace else to be and knew I enjoyed some time alone. Still, I was unprepared for it.

I knew that weather affected my mood, and Oregon's weather could be depressing. I had never seen so much rain or so many dreary grey days. I tried to ignore them, but when I thought about my parents walking along the warm and sunny Malecón waterfront, I closed my eyes and yearned to be there.

The day had begun with a cool grey drizzle that continued all morning. The sky changed from charcoal to a deep slate color. I decided to go outdoors for a walk even though it was drizzling. So I put on my raincoat, hat and boots and headed out toward the nearby woods.

As I walked, I let my angry tears mingle with the raindrops. The pain in my heart came from my feelings of helplessness and hopelessness. I was not in control of getting my parents out of Cuba. I was not even in control of my life here. I knew I had to let this frustration go; I had to give it to God.

The rain became angry, whipping the trees in the forest. I heard the howling of the wind and turned back. And just at that moment, the feeling of being separated from my life unexpectedly ended; I felt a surge of peace and knew I could let my heart follow my hope.

15

September 8, 1961

I would turn thirteen in just a few days—a "teenager," which is a very important milestone in the United States. Almost like a rite of passage. I think it's comparable to turning fifteen in Cuba and other Latin countries, when we celebrate our *Quinceañera*, marking the transition from childhood to womanhood.

I had never spent a birthday without my family, including my cousins and grandparents. Now I'll only be with Diego and my temporary family. But the Rustins would make sure I had a good day, understanding how hard it will be for me.

Mr. and Mrs. Rustin always seem to understand what I wanted even before I said a word. I had once admired Annette's Pendleton pleated skirt, made in the town of Pendleton, Oregon. These skirts are expensive and beautiful, and very "Oregonian." A lot of Annette's friends had them, and several girls in my class do as well.

After dinner last night, I was presented a beautifully-wrapped gift for my birthday.

"But it's not for another week," I protested.

"We know, but because you will celebrate your birthday then, we wanted you to have this tonight. Perhaps you and Annette can both wear your Pendleton skirts that day," suggested Mrs. Rustin with twinkling eyes.

Annette giggled, and I knew she had been a part of this conspiracy. Opening the box cover, I found the most beautiful Pendleton woolen skirt I had ever seen. It was a forest green plaid reversible pleated skirt, with just a few red and white lines running diagonally through it. Annette's was similar, but hers was forest brown instead of green. I was so pleased I was speechless.

That's how this family is. They are generous beyond understanding and always trying to please each other. I had no idea that Americans were like this; in fact, some of my friends in Cuba wrote to ask me if they were the "imperialist Yankees" that they were rumored to be. I look forward to changing their viewpoints through my experiences.

September 16, 1961

So much is happening now. I had a great birthday celebration with my American family, and the following day with my girlfriends. Even though my birthday was on a Thursday and we had school the next day, the Rustins took all of us to see the musical "Around the World in Eighty Days" at the Portland Civic Theatre. It was so spectacular and I've been reliving the songs and dances all day long.

My two girlfriends—Karen Fredericks and Connie Borsting—and their parents took the three of us to a really nice restaurant in downtown Portland for dinner. Huber's is Portland's oldest restaurant, which opened in 1879. Its specialty is turkey. We all loved it.

But the highlight of my birthday celebration was the

ten-minute phone call to our home in Cuba, which had been secretly pre-arranged between the Rustins and my parents. A half hour before we left for the theater, the operator phoned us with our scheduled telephone call.

"*Feliz Cumpleaños a ti, felicidades a ti, Feliz Cumpleaños querida hija, Happy Birthday to you*," they sang in harmony when I picked up the phone.

"O Mami, Papi, how did you time this so perfectly?" I asked, feeling the tears burning behind my eyes. "I am indeed having a happy day, and this is the best surprise," I stammered.

"Well, it has been about a month since we've talked, and we saved for this important phone call," answered my Papi. "It's such a joy to hear your voice. How is Diego?"

"I'm right here, Papi," interrupted my brother, snatching the phone from my hand. "We're going to the theater this evening to celebrate," he added. "We're going to see "Around the World in Eighty Days." His big brown eyes were shining. "Oh, and we can go to Sunday school now at our church because our English is better. So we'll be with kids our age instead of grown-ups."

He and my parents spoke for a few minutes, and then he handed me the phone.

I asked how things were going in Cuba, since I'd been hearing bits and pieces about Castro. "Oh, *hijita*, they are different now; more difficult, but your Mami and I are managing." Papi spoke carefully, in case soldiers were listening.

"Are you still working as a pharmacist?" I wondered.

"No, they closed my office three weeks ago. But I paint houses and fix roofs, and my back is still strong. That is how I keep in shape, and I also give your mother time to do her shopping and cooking."

I felt a sense of anxiety pulling on my shoulders but

ignored it. Mami took over the phone call. "Lili, are you wearing short skirts now? I see the photos of American girls and they look so short."

"No, Mami, here we don't because it's cooler now. And no make-up yet, so don't worry," I grinned at Annette, who had encouraged me to try lipstick.

"And no high heels, my girl. What about those little heels you wore on the airplane?"

I laughed out loud. "Ay, Mami, one of those heels broke the day we arrived in Miami. In fact, walking through the airport after we landed."

My mother giggled, "What a waste of money. *Te lo dije,*" she added smugly. (I told you so).

I heard Mami's voice choking. "What's wrong, Mami?"

"I was thinking of the day you were born; the happiness you brought into our lives. I never dreamed I would have to spend your birthday away from you, but I can stand this because I know you and Diego are safe, and with wonderful people who care for you." She was sobbing quietly, but I could hear it.

"Mami, I forgot to tell you that your birthday card also arrived today. It's been a wonderful day, filled with happy things. And hearing your voices almost makes it perfect."

It was time to hang up. My parents promised to join us soon. With a heavy sigh, I told them I believed them, while tucking "home" inside my heart with the memory of their love.

16

October 28, 1961

School was going well, and Diego and I had made some good friends. We felt much more comfortable now as students in a typical American school. But more news from Cuba was beginning to reach us. My best friend Connie brought me a newspaper article that someone had sent her mother. It was from *The Yuma Daily Sun*, written on September 29, 1961 and entitled: "*Firing Squads Have Only Started, Declares Castro.*" It was a horrible account of the savage murders in our beloved homeland.

"Is this true, Liliana?" she whispered, as we huddled over the article during lunch break.

"I don't know, Connie, but it may be. My parents cannot speak much about what is going on when they write or phone us, because the Castro Regime has soldiers spying everywhere." My chest tightened, and I found it harder to breathe. What would happen to my family in Cuba? I was angry, frightened, but unwilling to lie to myself about the reality of my country. No matter what happened, I knew I would carry Cuba inside me for the rest of my life.

Things were also heating up in school. One of my classmates had started picking on me. It started innocently enough—rolling her eyes when she heard me talk in class or in the lunch room. Then she asked me why I had such a stupid accent. I ignored all of that until the day she became much bolder on the bus.

"Hey, Cubana girl, how does it feel being the 'pity project' of the town?"

I was too shocked to answer, but Connie jumped up and faced her. "Are you jealous, Olivia, because Lili gets much more attention than you?"

"Jealous? Of that tamale? You must be kidding," she snickered, tossing back her hair as she passed us to find her seat in the back. She sat down with her mean friends. They spoke loudly enough to make sure we could hear them discussing us.

"Hey, don't pay any attention to her," advised Connie, turning in her seat to see my reaction. "She's just angry that the boy she likes is always looking at you in class."

"What are you saying, Connie? Who?"

"Russ Marvin. Don't you think he's cute?"

I had truly not noticed him, but decided I would now. "Connie, what does she mean by 'pity project'?" Even though I didn't fully understand what this meant, I knew it was an insult and I was humiliated.

"Liliana, she's a mean person who nobody really likes. Don't let her get to you. Ignore her."

For a few days, I allowed my insecurities to determine my behavior. Then I decided to have a conversation with Russ Marvin instead, and he turned out to be a very nice guy, handsome too. If it bothered Olivia that he preferred to talk to me, that was just "icing on the cake," as I heard Connie say once.

A few days later I asked Diego if he had been "picked on" or "bullied." He had no idea what that meant, but after I explained it to him, he shook his head. "I don't think so. Oh, I guess once a kid called me a 'spic,' but since I didn't know what it meant, I remembered it and asked a friend later."

"And did it stop?" I asked, worried about how Diego would deal with such prejudice. I didn't know that slang word, and later would ask Annette to explain it.

"Yep, and I still play sports with him at school, so I guess he's forgotten about it."

"What grade is he in?"

"He's in the fourth grade, so we really don't do much together. Hey Lili, I have to go meet Sebastian in a few minutes to bike into town." He grinned and sprinted away to change. He seemed to be handling it much better than I was.

Another girlfriend from Cuba sent me a letter telling me that my parents had requested exit visas. Then she added: *So now they're always being watched.* If she had intended to comfort me, she failed miserably.

When my parents called again I asked them about it. They downplayed the surveillance matter but admitted that they were doing everything they could to leave, including applications for exit visas. Mami even whispered the word "visas" in case their conversation was recorded. They said they hadn't told us when they applied because those visas took months or even years to be approved. They chose not to mention that they had been put on the "Counter-Revolutionary" list, and it was doubtful they would ever be approved. Knowing that must have broken their hearts.

Unaware of that list, I clung to hope and prayer. My parents didn't give up, even knowing they were considered "discontents or rebels." The important thing was that we all kept our faith.

At ten o'clock one evening, Mrs. Rustin walked into our

bedroom to tell me that my parents were on the phone. Concerned about the late hour, I raced off to the kitchen.

"Mami? Is everything all right?" I asked nervously.

"*Sí mi hijita*." (Yes my daughter). But I could hear the quiet sniffles through her words.

"Then why are you calling so late, and sounding so sad?"

She cleared her throat, and I heard my father speaking to her in the background.

"My exit visa was approved this morning. I have just seven days to leave the country or I have to stay indefinitely in Cuba."

"What? You are coming here? You and Papi will be able to leave?" I felt so happy I wanted to scream. "Do you need money for tickets? Diego and I have some saved up and . . ."

Papi took the phone from her hands. "Your mother is very excited and happy, but she is so choked up that I must tell you the rest of the story," his breathing sounded forced.

"What Papi? Should I go get Diego? He's sleeping," I blurted, now holding my breath.

"Lili, let him sleep. I will tell you and you can explain it to him tomorrow. I was not granted the exit visa . . . yet, because I'm, well, I'm still required to work for the country here. I will find a way to get to you. But you must encourage your mother to go while she still can."

Now I was crying. "But Papi, she won't want to leave you. How can I convince her?"

He said quietly, "Just tell her you and Diego need her. Tell her she must join you. We have the money for her ticket, and I know God will provide for the rest."

I knew that too, and a sweet peace floated down and settled over me. "Put Mami back on please, Papi." I told him, calmer now. "I will talk to her." He gave her the phone.

"Mami, you must come. We will work everything out

here. I'll speak to the Rustins tomorrow, and we'll find a way. Remember, you are not choosing between your husband and your children. You are helping to build a future for us all."

When we hung up, Annette and her mother came to me with troubled eyes. They could see my heart was breaking and opened their arms, folding me into a gentle hug while I sobbed.

When I had quieted down, I told them about the phone call. "My mother received her exit visa but my father did not. The Cuban authorities are doing this on purpose, trying to destroy our family because my parents have not been loyal to the Regime. I hate them all!" I screamed, bursting into tears once again.

We wept together. After a few moments, Mr. Rustin walked into the room and we discussed the phone call with him.

He quickly told us what he had decided. "Your mother will live with us, and we'll all pray that your father will be allowed to follow her soon." Dear Mr. Rustin. He provided the perfect solution with clarity and strength. Now I believed that we had nothing to worry about.

Everyone got right to work preparing for our mother's arrival. She would have her own bedroom, formerly part of a large office space. Annette, Mrs. Rustin and I went shopping to buy Mami a basic wardrobe, since she'd only be allowed to pack a few outfits. If the blouses, skirts and dresses we bought didn't suit her, she could exchange them for different clothes. I prayed that the airport soldiers would not confiscate her wedding ring or her mother's pearls.

When the day finally arrived, we got to the airport early enough to get a snack. Annette and Sebastian decided to stay home, so Diego and I could spend more uninter-rupted time with her.

Would Mami think we'd changed? I knew Diego had grown taller, but was I the same? I still wore my hair like before, but maybe my face and body were different after six months? I felt different. I felt that somewhere between my journey from Cuba and this moment of reuniting in the airport, I had grown up. I hoped my mother didn't think I'd forgotten everything she had taught me.

Diego seemed calmer than I was. He wasn't even fidget-ing. Maybe he'd grown up too. But he was still too young! Would Mami recognize us? My thoughts were flying all over the place. I felt butterflies in my stomach as we hur-ried to the arrival gate.

People began walking toward us. When Diego bolted away from us, we knew he had spotted her.

"Mami, Mami," he screamed. "Ay, Mami, you are here!"

She dropped her bag and pulled him into her open arms. They held each other for a very long time.

Then her eyes searched for me and she saw the tears running down my cheeks. Her smile was radiant. I walked toward her as if through heavy molasses.

Mami threw her arms around me, kissing away my tears. "*Ay, mi hijita. ¡Que hermosa estás!* (My little daughter, how beautiful you are!)" Her voice was thick and musical, just as I remembered it.

When I saw several people watching us, I remembered the Rustins.

I turned around to see them wiping away their own happy tears. Taking their hands in mine, I introduced them to my mother.

"Mami, these are the wonderful people who have cared for us since we arrived in Oregon: Robin and Charlie

Rustin. " I choked on my emotion. "Mr. and Mrs. Rustin, meet our mother."

Mami went to each one and hugged them, laughing and crying at the same time.

"Thank you, mil gracias," she said over and over. "Thank you for loving my children."

We drove home talking about things less important than our biggest concern: our father's situation. We could discuss that later.

We wouldn't know for a few more days that Cuba was changing very quickly. We hadn't heard that three days after my birthday, Castro's government had expelled one hundred-thirty priests and other religious workers, shipping them to Spain on a steamer called *Covadonga*. The Catholic clergy had been reduced from about one thousand in 1960 to two hundred thirty-three in 1961.

No one had told us that government employees had been rushing into churches and yelling Revolutionary slogans during Mass.

Or that on August 6th, all Cuban airports and seaports had been closed while every Cuban was forced to exchange their pesos for newly printed currency. Heads of family could only exchange two hundred pesos.

As the truth came out in bits and pieces, it became painfully obvious that we wouldn't be able to return to our country in the near future. We needed to get Papi out of Cuba and here with us as quickly as possible, before we no longer could. Only then could we begin another life together in this country. I believed that one day we would call it "home."

17

December 10, 1961

James could not remember ever seeing Father Walsh so angry. The hand holding the phone was trembling and his voice had become strident.

"He really said that: that he's not only a Socialist, but he's actually a Marxist-Leninist and has been from the beginning of the Revolution?" His voice shook as he scribbled notes and held the phone against the other shoulder.

"Oh, I see. Hmm. So Fidel thought that hiding his being a communist would help his Revolution succeed, did he?" Father Walsh's face tightened, and his body stiffened. He was silent for a long while.

James couldn't look away. Something important was going on here.

"Yes, thank you, Father. I will ring off now and share this news with the others."

He replaced the receiver, suddenly infinitely weary. "James, tomorrow Castro will proclaim a new law requiring Cuban nationals to obtain exit permits to leave their own country and entry permits if they want to return." He was almost whispering as he walked to the center of the room and stopped, slowly shaking his head.

"Dear Lord . . . why would he do that?" James Baker asked, his stomach cramping.

Father Walsh raised a brow. "Maybe to keep the currency from leaving the country? Remember, just four months ago he cancelled the existing Cuban peso, issued a new currency printed in Czechoslovakia, and allowed every citizen to exchange only two hundred pesos. But he permitted up to ten thousand additional pesos to be deposited in a personal account in the nationalized banks. So some Cubans still have money in their accounts."

James nodded. "Yes Father, but they can only withdraw one hundred pesos per month, even in the existing accounts before he changed the peso."

Father Walsh shook his head emphatically. "They are most likely using that money to send Cuban students behind the Iron Curtain." He walked over to his desk and opened the top drawer, pulling out a newspaper. "Have you seen this article from the *Revolución*, Cuba's largest newspaper? Read it. It says over two thousand Cuban students are now studying in Russia."

James took a few moments to read this. Then his gaze met Father Walsh's. "This is heart-breaking to read, and also to recall what *Avance* wrote about the Youth Organizations, now run by the Revolutionaries and influencing children just five years old! And to think of the pressure they're applying to those same students we once taught, and also to their younger siblings!"

"Yes, James. And those who do not participate face public ridicule and abuse." Facing James, he put his left hand on his friend's shoulder. "I forgot for a moment that you knew many of these children. I share your pain and I'm so sorry."

They stood quietly, seeking inspiration. Finally, James spoke.

"Father Walsh, I also worry about our mutual friends in

Cuba's underground movement. The failure of the Bay of Pigs invasion has left them in disarray, and U.S. support seems to have disappeared."

"Let not your heart be troubled, my friend. Let's wait to see how well Robert Kennedy's *Operation Mongoose* program works out. I have great faith in its leader, General Edward Lansdale."

"I will confess that I know very little about the anti-Castro operation, but like you, I feel optimistic, knowing that Lansdale was an Air Force colonel," James added.

"Aye, James. Going back to the subject of Cuban refugees, our own *Operation Pedro Pan* keeps growing uncontrollably, and I'm constantly in search of even more housing."

"I know, Father. But sending the Pedro Pans to other states is starting to open up for us, isn't it?"

Father Walsh's face broke into a grin. "Thank the Lord for the many Catholic Archdioceses around the country that have stepped up to help. As they place Catholic children themselves, they're finding homes for others through Protestant and Jewish organizations."

He stepped from behind the desk and motioned to another easy chair. "Please sit down, James. Let me show you some new temporary shelters."

Reaching for a large, well-worn notebook, he flipped through the pages.

"You know we opened Matecumbe last July. Father Francisco Palá is doing a great job with those difficult teenage boys," he chuckled.

"Yes, they are the boys aged fifteen to eighteen, right?"

"More or less. We still have several younger ones. But as you know, the capacity is for three hundred fifty and even with tents, we're completely overloaded. We're trying to move some of them to smaller places. The Cuban Home for Boys on SW 15th Road has just closed, and some of the boys and I will move to Saint Raphael's."

"What will happen to the Cuban Home for Boys?" asked James.

"It's being renamed Whitehall, and we'll keep about twenty boys there. Because the Jesuit Brothers are taking it over, it will also be called the Jesuit's Boys' Home. I trust Father Jesús Nuevo will do a good job there."

"So you're moving into Saint Raphael's?"

"Yes, and as you know, that's not a transient shelter like most of the others. I must keep a permanent home with those children who stay until their parents can arrive. Oh, and Whitehall will be run the same way."

James heard the smile in Father Walsh's comments. "Father, I've not seen Saint Raphael's yet. When would be a good time to visit?"

"Anytime, James. I'd love to show you around. Just give me a shout. Ray McCraw will arrive soon, and he has impeccable credentials."

"And Florida City? That one also opened in October for the younger boys and the girls, right?"

"Yes, and it's the furthest one from the city. I believe it will be the largest as well. Again, I have a great administrator in Father Salvador De Cistierna, and the Sisters of St. Phillip Neri from Spain are very kind, yet strict, with the girls. It seems to be running smoothly so far."

"I heard you have set up a very large tent for Mass. How is that working out?"

Father Walsh laughed. "Oh my, much better than I'd imagined. The children love having Sunday service where they live, so they have more time to play. They also use the tent to escape the Florida sun on other days."

"Isn't it close to Homestead and the Air Force Base? There's also a large park nearby as I recall."

"You have an excellent memory, James. Yes, it turned out to be a good shelter, but we have close to five hundred children now, and definitely require more staff."

"By staff, you mean foster parents, don't you? I seem to remember apartments there, where the children live with their foster parents, usually Cuban couples. That sounds like a more homelike environment than some of the other shelters."

"Yes, they have foster parents." He paused and rolled his eyes. "Oh, and now they have a new plan: weekly dances rotated among the various shelters. I was going to suggest having a Christmas party, but then we'd need to do one in each shelter, and I don't have enough energy left this year to pull that off." He smiled, but his Irish good looks had suffered a little from all the work.

James smiled back. "I can see that you have a lot to handle, Father Walsh. But if anyone can do it and keep his kindness and good humor, you are the man."

"Thank you, James. But I have so many other people to thank, including you. As long as you continue to help with the paperwork and advise us on the important decisions for *Operation Pedro Pan*, I know we'll be able to keep this organization above water." Smiling again, he clasped his friend's hand warmly. "And the good Lord will give us the strength."

"Amen," James answered softly.

As he turned and headed for the door, Father Walsh was reaching into his pocket.

"Oh, I almost forgot, James. I received a letter for both of us and George from Liliana and Diego Escobár." A warm smile spread across his face. "Their mother arrived in early

November, and they are still waiting for news about their father's visa. They're confident, though, he will arrive in time for Christmas."

"That's wonderful news, Father! They're in Oregon, aren't they?" asked James, pulling the letter out of the envelope. "I'll write back and ask if they have snow. I always teased them about going to cold winters."

Father Walsh nodded cheerfully. "For a morning that started so badly, it has ended well. Thank you, James, for helping me rediscover my joy."

18

December 12, 1961

Our mother was adjusting quite well to her new life in Oregon. She enrolled in evening English classes twice a week at the nearby Presbyterian Church. We could walk her there, and one of us would wait and do our homework until her class ended. Several other Spanish speakers studied with her, so she made a few friends.

Of course she missed our father, but we talked to him about once a week, thanks to the Rustins. He assured us he was doing fine alone and working hard to get his visa waiver. All we could do was wait. With Mami here, an unexpected sense of peace settled in.

Meanwhile, Diego, Annette, Sebastian and I couldn't wait for Christmas break. It would start after three more school days and last for two weeks. Diego's class had prepared a Christmas program, starring him as Joseph, the father of Jesus. He was especially excited to have Mami in the audience for that evening's performance.

Mrs. Rustin had been taking our mother to the grocery store each week to buy ingredients for some of our favorite Cuban dishes. Of course, Mami couldn't always find what she would have found in Havana, especially the spices, so she tried her best to substitute. But honestly, the meals were always delicious, because Mami prepared them. And she taught Mrs. Rustin how to cook some of the dishes the family most enjoyed.

Mami made dinner once or twice a week; Annette, Mrs. Rustin and I chopped vegetables and learned from her. Those times together were filled with so much laughter, and I felt really close to being completely "happy." Then I closed my eyes and thought, *Papi, when you come . . .*

I really believed it would happen soon.

On the weekends Annette and I made breakfast. On Saturdays we cooked Cuban or Spanish foods that Mami had taught me in Havana. I introduced the Rustin family to a real Cuban breakfast of *café con leche* and ham and cheese *croquetas.*

"Croquetas" are breadcrumb-coated fried rolls made of entree leftovers (chicken, sausage, ham, etc.) and usually topped with béchamel sauce. Then on Sundays we made a full American breakfast, with bacon and eggs, toast, fruit and whatever else we had in the kitchen.

Another one of my mother's skills was knitting. I knew she was secretly knitting shawls for Annette and Robin Rustin and warm scarves for Sebastian and Charlie Rustin. Diego and I wondered if we'd also be gifted one of her beautiful creations.

"Lili, I looked in her room and can't find anything for us, so who knows?" he giggled.

"Diego, shame on you. Why spoil a surprise?"

Then I remembered the most memorable surprise Mami had ever given me—the day she arrived in Oregon. Not seeing the diamond ring on her finger at the airport, once we were alone I asked if they had confiscated it. She laughed gleefully and said, "No, *querida* (dear). I out-smarted them and sewed it into this." She removed her hair band and opened up a seam. There was her lovely wedding ring. I was so relieved they had not found it. I asked about the pearls and she said she left them with my father.

The Christmas program was so much fun. Every performance was wonderful, especially Diego's. The drinks and desserts that followed made Sebastian and Diego very happy.

As we walked to the car, the air was brisk and turning colder-exactly how I always pictured American Christmas weather to be.

"Mami, will you miss spending Christmas in Cuba?" I asked her later that evening.

She hugged me. "Perhaps the traditions, but we can always do them here as well. I miss not being with your father," she said solemnly, "but I am so grateful to be with Diego and you. Keep praying that things will change and that Papi will soon be here with us." Her sweet smile was sadly uncertain.

We'd received a very unsettling letter from my father. He wrote: *How many souls have been lost by people risking everything to find a better life? How many people have stared across the ocean, yearning for something they can't have: their children, their traditions, their country, even their air and soil?* Mami read it and cried, then showed it to me later.

Papi normally didn't speak about the situation in Cuba or express his longings so it meant so much that he had opened up his heart to us.

"I don't think we should share this with Diego, but I believe you will understand his desperate state of mind. Lili, please tell me you still believe he'll be here by Christmas."

I touched her cool cheeks. "Yes, Mami. I still believe that." Then I hugged her tightly.

"I have an idea," I told her. "Let's include one of our Christmas traditions into this Christmas holiday with the Rustins. I'll let you choose which one."

She nodded and held me close. "I think I know which one we'll do, and I'll surprise you all."

December 21, 1961

The phone rang in the middle of the night. Mami had an extension in her room and knew instantly that it was for her.

"*Aló? Eres tú Francisco?* (Hello, is that you, Francisco?)"

"*Sí, mi amor. Soy yo. Y tengo noticias.* (Yes, my love. It's me . . . and I have news)."

By this time, I was wide awake and dashing to her room. "Mami," I whispered. "When is he coming?"

I watched the tears spill from her eyes, then felt them fill my own. I knew it! Papi had obtained his visa!

"Speak with him, *querida*. Let him tell you himself." She reached for her tissues.

"Papi, please tell me you are coming now," I implored him. "We need you so much." I could feel my body shivering. He had not yet spoken a word.

Finally. "Yes, my darling. I will be there for Christmas, just as you predicted," he told me, his voice cracking with emotion. Then his sweet laughter was followed by a joyful "Aleluya!"

"Praise be to God, Papi. How did you get the visa?"

"I'll explain the details later. I have friends in the

underground who helped me. I arrive on Flight 24 from Chicago in two days. I've already sent you a telegram with all the information."

Sobbing with happiness, I handed the telephone back to Mami. Then I ran into the boys' room to wake up Diego.

Through my own blurred eyes, I gave Diego the wonderful news. He wiped his cheeks with the back of his hand. Wrapping our arms around each other, we could feel that very soon we'd been together and happy at last.

19

December 24, 1961

Mami prepared a very special Christmas Eve dinner, with Papi as her assistant. They talked non-stop and had so much to chat about. No one else was allowed in the kitchen while she prepared the "Cuban surprise" she had chosen.

Papi was thinner now: "That's how much I missed Mami's cooking," he joked. He ate with our grandmother, and had only two meals a day. He didn't want to talk about Cuba's sad situation, and we respected that. Our mother told us that time would heal all wounds, and we were so busy enjoying his return to the family that we didn't ask those questions.

The Rustins continued to make him and the rest of us feel we belonged there. I know Papi and Mr. Rustin discussed how he would get his pharmaceutical license certified in the United States, but first we needed to decide where we'd live. Everything else could wait until after the New Year.

Every Cuban looks forward to our traditional "*Noche Buena*" (Christmas Eve) dinner, and now Mami was adding the final touches. Typically, we roast a whole suckling pig, called *lechón*, outdoors over hot coals. This year my parents were preparing it in the oven. *Yuca*, or *cassava*, one of our favorite vegetables—similar to a sweet potato—was unavailable, so Mami baked regular sweet potatoes instead. Her black beans over rice were exactly like we ate in Havana, accompanied by *tostones* (small discs of fried plantain with salt). As for dessert, her *flan* custard was simply the best any of us had ever tasted.

The dining table was beautifully decorated—a Christmas tablecloth, linen napkins, Christmas china and crystal glasses—and moved near the Christmas tree. In all the excitement we hadn't bought a tree. So the day after Papi's arrival, the men and boys went out to cut one down in the nearby forest. We girls trimmed it late yesterday evening until it glowed with ornaments, lights and tinsel. This serene and lovely atmosphere put us all in the Christmas spirit.

We younger ones agreed to draw names from a hat and purchase a Christmas gift for that person. We knew the parents would find something for all of us, and we had already bought them gifts from our allowance money. But I wasn't sure if Mami and Papi would have money to do that.

Diego peeked mischievously between the branches as I was watering the tree and gave me his secret grin. "I know how Papi got his money!"

"What money, Diego?" I was preoccupied with not spilling any water.

"How he got here, how he bribed the airport officials, how . . ."

"What did you say?"

"Well, Papi and Mami were talking behind their closed door and I sat outside the room in the hall and listened. First, he sold some of her jewelry to pay for the ticket to Miami and then to Oregon. Then, he paid off someone he knew in the underground movement to get the visa faster, and then he had to give the soldiers or someone extra money to get on the plane." He smirked, extremely proud of his information.

"You spied on them, Diego!"

"Did not. I couldn't see them so it wasn't really spying."

I laughed. "How do you know he still had money to bring with him?"

"Because I heard him tell Mami he hid it 'on his person.' But I don't know what that means."

"*Eres un loco, hermanito.* (You are crazy, little brother.) But I love you anyway." I explained what it meant to hide something *on his person.*

Leaving the room, he glanced over his shoulder. "Oh, and I saw what you wrapped this afternoon, but I won't tell Sebastian," he said, laughing.

It was a real-family style dinner and conversation flowed freely. Mami's English had improved, and Papi had always spoken it pretty well, so there was no language barrier. It felt like Christmas Eve in our Cuban home, with delicious Cuban cuisine aromas and my parents sitting side by side.

Everything was perfect, and Mami looked so pleased. Our dear Papi could not stop smiling.

The evening was our magical miracle as we welcomed a new season into our lives. The next year would cleanse away the pain and sorrow from this past year. The family I loved was here with me.

"This moment marks the beginning of what's to come," pronounced Mr. Rustin, as if he were reading my thoughts. "We look forward to the good things we will share, we are grateful for the reunion of the Escobárs, and we pray for the future of our countries." He held up a glass and we did the same. "God bless us all," he smiled.

"And thank you for everything, Lord, especially for this joyful reunion with our children," added Mami.

Papi also had a toast. "Here's to the wonderful Rustin family, who is now our family as well. And to the United States of America, the country that took us in and offered us freedom."

Everyone at the table lifted a glass and gave thanks. We realized this was a turning point in all of our lives, a transformation that none of us would ever forget.

I closed my eyes and for a long moment, I ached for the Cuba I loved. It was a fleeting remembrance, and I wondered if my family felt it as well behind the cheerful faces and laughing voices.

I silently offered a prayer. *Ay, mi querida Cuba, I pray for you.*

PART TWO

Rodolfo & Agustín

20
April 12, 1962

Our car stopped under a roughly lettered sign: *Matecumbe*. Padre Palá got out and opened a shabby wooden gate, returned to the car and we continued down a dirt road toward a rustic cabin.

"Matecumbe is an Indian name," Padre Palá told us as we bumped ahead. "Florida natives living in this area were converted to Christianity by eighteenth-century Cuban missionaries. After years as a summer retreat for priests, this became a summer camp for Catholic children.

I squinted through the darkness to get a feeling for what living here would be like.

The car came to a standstill at the front door. "We're here. Let's go inside the main office and get you registered. Then, if you're hungry, I can try to find something for you to eat, even though the kitchen is closed." The priest unloaded our small cardboard suitcases from the trunk.

Register? Again? How many times had we already filled out paperwork? I complained to myself.

Meanwhile my calm younger brother, Agustín, followed the priest into a small front parlor and sat down at a small table. I asked if we could eat soon.

"Yes, I'll go to the kitchen to see what I can rustle up. Sit down, Rodolfo, and fill out your questionnaire, okay?"

After the flight, the long drive to this poorly-lit log cabin, and the lack of food, I realized I had a terrible headache and was in no mood to fill out more paperwork. I just closed my eyes and enjoyed the quiet. Just as I was calming down, the priest returned with two glasses of milk and a plate of sardines.

"Sardines?" I yelled. "That's what we feed our dogs and cats in Cuba!" Then I noticed saltine crackers on a plate and felt a little better—that's how hungry I was. I devoured the food even though I felt insulted.

"You'll have a proper breakfast tomorrow morning. This is all we have for now," he answered, noticing my blank form.

"Rodolfo, the sooner you complete your questionnaire, the sooner you'll get to bed." After throwing him a dirty look I filled it out quickly and carelessly, then put it on top of Agustin's carefully completed form.

We walked down a path through tropical trees with the help of a small flashlight. Hearing a hissing sound, I asked a little nervously if there were any snakes here.

"Yes, and soon you'll learn to tell which ones are poisonous," he answered casually.

We stepped into a larger log cabin and were told to assemble our own cots. We saw other campers asleep in two rows of bunk beds against the walls. All we had were Army cots in the middle of the large room.

"When do we get our bunk beds too?" I demanded, looking around for a spot to put our cardboard suitcases, and finding nothing.

"Tomorrow several boys leave for their foster homes. Right now we're completely full, but we'll have bunk beds for you then."

Agustín struggled to unfold his cot; I helped him. Then

we fell into a deep sleep, hoping things would look a little better in the morning.

Breakfast was horrible. They served us dry toast, corn flakes and milk. Then we were taken to a very large tent—just pitched the day before, Padre Palá explained, and lined with double-bunk beds. We each found an unoccupied bunk and claimed it, covering the mattresses with the sheets they gave us. I also saw some small lockers where I stowed our suitcases.

Agustín was hopeful. "Rodolfo, *todo tranquilo* (be calm). Let's try to make the best of what we're getting," he pleaded. "There's no point in being miserable, right?"

Who was I to try and take away his hope? "You are right, *hermanito (little brother)*. Let's have faith that we'll find a way to make the best of this," I grinned, tweaking his ear. "It's what Cubans are famous for, right?"

There was a large forest behind the tent. We stepped out the back door and looked into it more carefully. Dusty gilded sunlight was piercing holes in the evergreen canopy, and rich golden beams hit the forest's pine-needle carpet like spotlights. The hard blue sky was scattered with rainless white clouds. A slight breeze rustled through the trees, swinging the branches back and forth through the heat and humidity. It was beautiful, and I pointed it out to my brother.

"Here's proof that it will be better. Where have we ever seen such beauty? This plain camp may turn out to be heaven on earth. Who knows?" It had been too long since we shared a moment like this so we avoided bursting the bubble with conversation.

Then a tough-looking guy about my age walked up and tried to burst our bubble for us. "Welcome to Matecumbe, *El Infierno Verde.*"

"Why do you call it *The Green Hell?*" asked Agustín, shocked from our short reverie.

He grinned. "You'll know soon enough," he teased. "My name is Leonardo and I'm from Matanzas. Where did you guys come from?"

"We're from Santiago de Cuba—Rodolfo and Agustín Socarras," answered my well-mannered brother, nodding in my direction. "I'm Agustín. How long have you been here?"

"About six months now. I'm ready to get my *beca* and go live with a family."

I asked him, "What about your parents? Aren't they coming for you?"

His cocky expression faded, and he smiled sadly. "We all hope so, but the visa waivers are nearly impossible to get. Most of us end up living with families first."

On our way back to the main office to apply for our parents' visas, we could see more of Matecumbe in the daylight. We were excited to see an Olympic-sized swimming pool because we were good swimmers. Several trails led off into the thick forest behind it—which we'd soon get to know on the "nature walks." I was fascinated to realize the bark on the giant tree trunks was covered with blue-green lichens.

Later we had lunch with Leonardo and the others. He explained how to serve ourselves from large casserole dishes on the big table, and advised us to grab the pieces of fried chicken we wanted before somebody else got them.

"They just hired a new Cuban cook after many complaints about the tasteless American cuisine," he added. Along with the fried chicken we had black beans and rice.

Once we were seated, a shrill whistle sounded and a priest led us in a long blessing.

After staring hungrily at the food for so long, we could finally eat. Agustín and I were so hungry we ate everything on our plate and went back for seconds. The taste of home made us happy and full. Leonardo said to wait until we were dismissed as a group.

Leaving the lunch area, Leonardo's cocky expression returned as he recited the camp rules.

"No swimming in the pool without a counselor lifeguard. No sleeping in or walking around after hours. Don't forget to make your beds. Absolutely no fighting!"

"If you break any of these rules, there are consequences. You might not get your weekly allowance," he told us. "That means not being able to buy goodies in the camp canteen, or go to downtown Miami on the weekend with the rest of us."

"The worst punishment in *El Infierno Verde* is not being able to go to the weekend dances, to meet and dance the Salsa with the Pedro Pan girls." It sounded like a lot of "no's" and "not's" to me. His smile grew wider at our reaction to so many rules and punishments. Then he walked away.

Agustín and I met separately with social workers in the main office. Afterwards we compared notes.

"Agustín, did he ask you where you wanted to go?" I asked.

"Yeah, and I said '*back to Cuba*', but he didn't mean that, I guess."

"I told him we wanted to stay right here in Miami until our parents can come," I said. "And then he said that would depend on what living arrangements became available, but that they don't keep boys here forever. He told me they just closed up a high school program they had here, so we'd be going to public school soon. Oh, and here's the part I didn't like—he told me that sometimes they have to separate brothers, but that it's highly unusual."

Agustín took a step backward in alarm.

"That's not going to happen to us, *hermanito* (little brother). I won't let it."

"Rodolfo, he wanted to know when I'd turn fifteen, which luckily won't be long. He told me this camp is for boys aged fifteen to eighteen."

"Well, I just turned eighteen, so we're both okay," I smiled.

Later that afternoon we were given a short history of *Operation Pedro Pan*. Its founders James Baker and Father Walsh were originally asked to organize temporary lodging for about two hundred children. To keep this exodus a secret from Fidel Castro, they worked with trusted clergy in Cuba and prominent figures in the counter-revolution to form a network that obtained visas, passports, and airline tickets.

In less than a year and a half that number had risen to almost eight thousand. It was time to move the kids out of Miami and into homes and shelters across the country.

A boy named Miguel in our tent told us that it didn't always work out that way. "There aren't enough homes available, so some kids end up in orphanages, even though they can't be adopted. Others go to reform schools to wait for their parents. It's horrible, and they are very unhappy. But, we really don't have a say in the *becas* they give us, so all we can do is hope for the best."

My brother and I walked outside and stared at the moon. I reminded him it was the same moon we shared with Mamá and Papá in Santiago de Cuba. "Sharing it connects us, and makes me feel closer to them," I told him.

We sat down on a bench, and I started writing a letter to our parents. Not wanting them to worry, I told them only good things. I smiled as I noticed Agustín pulling out a piece of yellow paper he'd brought from Cuba. He would write his own version.

21

May 18, 1962

Matecumbe was supposed to be a structured place, but in reality we wandered about at will. There were too many of us to monitor carefully, so between the few classes offered to us, some cruel pranks were played on innocent boys, usually newcomers.

One afternoon on our way to dinner we heard a lot of shouting coming from the pool area. Agustín took off running, and I was close behind him.

"Hurry Rodolfo, it's Ramón! He's drowning in the pool!"

Ramón, fully clothed, was kicking furiously in the deep end of the pool and screaming for help. With no staff nearby, his tormentors were hooting gleefully at his terror. I plunged in to help him and realized his hands had been tied behind his back, so he couldn't swim to safety.

"Hey *compañero* (buddy), we were just going to fish him out," one of them shouted as I pulled Ramón through water to the side of the pool.

I was furious. Fifteen-year old Ramón, still sputtering and gagging in fear, fought me as I untied his hands and pulled off his wet shirt. "Easy, Ramón. You're safe." Agustín tossed him his dry shirt to change into.

Turning to the group of bullies, I read them the "riot

act." "Does this make you feel bigger and better, *cabrones* (bastards)? You get your kicks picking on younger kids? Your stupid prank could have cost him his life!" Anger and sadness twisted violently inside me.

I was repulsed by their arrogance and ashamed they were fellow Cubans. They walked away laughing, because they knew nothing would happen to them.

This was the first violent dunking incident I saw, but not the last. Sadly, it was almost a ritual for many newcomers at Matecumbe.

Agustín and I studied English with the same teacher, but at different times of day. Matecumbe offered intensive English lessons to prepare us for relocation. We both had crushes on Señora Margarita Oteiza, a young widow who used to teach at Ruston Academy in Havana.

On our first day she told us she had started with *Operation Pedro Pan* when Señor George asked her to pick up children at the airport. But it quickly broke her heart to try and comfort the little ones—many clung to her, sobbing tears of despair. So she decided to teach English at Matecumbe.

She arrived in an old car with books and a blackboard. We didn't even have a classroom and usually met outdoors, near a pine tree with a sign that read: *Mrs. Oteiza's room.* When it rained, she would hold classes in the bus, sitting in the driver's seat and facing us. Everyone paid attention and did their best to earn her praise.

My classmates said her husband had been killed during the Bay of Pigs invasion by Fidel's army. But nobody had the courage to ask her if that was true.

She was beautiful, and we boys were as obedient and respectful as we could be. We thought she looked like a movie star and noticed that she walked like a ballerina.

Since we knew we would go to the local public high school in September, we often skipped other classes and nobody seemed to notice. There were just too many of us, and too few staff members to monitor us.

There were not enough bathrooms or showers for three hundred of us, so some students decided to use the outdoor showers by the swimming pool. Some of the older boys also snuck out after lights-out, and who knew what shenanigans they staged.

Swimming, hiking and playing soccer helped us forget our hardships. We all looked forward to Friday night dances with the girls. On Saturdays we usually took the bus into Miami, leaving early in the morning and returning late at night. Anyone with family or friends in Miami could spend the weekend with them. We were once invited by two new friends to join them and their family for a weekend visit. Some campers would visit siblings in other camps, too.

Alberto Ochoa, my new friend, was fun to hang out with. His younger brother, Sergio, got along well with Agustín. They would come along on our Saturday adventures into Miami. One Saturday we got up early to walk to Miami Beach.

"How far is it, Rodolfo?" asked Agustín. "Shouldn't we ride the bus?"

"Not too far, *hermanito* (little brother). It will be an adventure, and some exercise too. We can always ride the bus back."

Walking gave the four of us a chance to get to know each other better. The Ochoa brothers were *Havaneros* (from Havana); we were from the other side of Cuba. But we got along well and enjoyed chatting and joking.

In Miami Beach we stopped to buy hamburgers from

a Cuban attorney at his small stand. He told us he abandoned everything to escape Castro. As we sat on a bench and enjoyed the burgers, he and I talked about our favorite Cuban musicians: Celia Cruz, Machito and Olga Guillot. It made me feel very homesick.

Walking further along North Beach, we admired its Art Deco hotels and observed the people. We laughed at all the old couples sunning themselves with olive oil by little pools.

"Hey guys, look! There's the Fontainebleau Hotel," Alberto exclaimed. "Isn't that where the rich and famous performers sing and dance?"

"Yes, and it has Sammy Davis Jr.'s photo on the billboard," I added. "He and Frank Sinatra might be performing tonight!" Someone at the camp had heard about that on our television.

Alberto's eyes widened. "I really like their new album with the song *Me and My Shadow*. Oh, and then there's *What Kind of Fool Am I?* It reminds me of the *Cubanita* girlfriend I left behind." His sadness made me miss home and remember my loved ones in Cuba.

Now the younger boys joined in the excitement. "Maybe we can get their autographs! Let's go in," insisted Sergio.

Alberto and I exchanged amused glances and nodded. "*Vamos* (Let's go)!"

In the lobby, we nearly bumped into Sammy Davis Jr. and his five security men dressed in black. A small crowd of women at the exit shoved papers and small pamphlets into his face, begging for autographs. Others called out his name and took pictures. He waved to them all and smiled broadly. "Maybe later, after the show," he promised, before ducking into a large white limousine parked outside the hotel door.

And just like that, we had our story! No pictures or autographs, but we had seen him and heard his voice. We were sure to be the envy of the boys at dinner tonight.

That same evening, at about ten o'clock, Alberto sat on the edge of my bunk, where I was reading. His eyes were red and his voice filled with tears.

"*Qué pasó, compadre?* (What happened, buddy)?" I asked him.

"*Malditas noticias de mi amigo!* (Damned horrible news about my friend)!" he sputtered, his face rigid and angry.

He told me in starts and stops about a letter he had just been given. His friend Eduardo had finally written two months after leaving Matecumbe. Unfortunately, Eduardo had received a bad *beca*—an orphanage in Philadelphia, where he was forced to wash floors and clean toilets. If they didn't like his work, the nuns would beat him and make him sleep on a cold floor.

The other boys were wild and carried knives, often threatening him just to pick fights. The only thing he liked was going to the local high school, but many of those students called him a "thug" because he lived in an orphanage.

"Tell Padre Palá," I told him. "Or better yet, let's go see Father Walsh." I couldn't understand how this could possibly happen. Our parents had sent us to this country for freedom, only to be treated like that? Shouldn't the *Operation Pedro Pan* staff know about this?

Alberto went to Padre Palá, who notified Father Walsh. As far as we knew, nothing was done; not because they didn't want to help, but because they didn't have the staff. The program had grown so large and so decentralized that the Catholic Welfare Bureau could no longer track the living conditions of all the children once they left the camps in Florida.

It got me thinking about Agustín and me. Where would we go while waiting for our parents' arrival? Would we have a say in where we went? Based on what was happening at Matecumbe, chances are we wouldn't.

22

July 10, 1962

Father Walsh knew that a Fourth of July celebration would be special for any newly arrived boy or girl in the Pedro Pan program.

He hoped it would be a chance for them to celebrate the opportunities that living in the United States could give them: the freedom for education, work, pursuing their dreams and perhaps sharing these experiences with their families one day.

It would be a celebration of the thirteen colonies coming together to establish a great nation, where generations of immigrants were given a chance to prosper and work hard to help their families. A chance to come together with new friends to make *carne asada* or hamburgers, to watch the fireworks, and celebrate independence from an oppressive government and hope for a better future.

Since the holiday fell on a Wednesday, the children would observe the festivities the following weekend. The Catholic Welfare Bureau had organized parties in two of the shelters for Saturday afternoon, and in three others on Sunday. That way, everyone could celebrate with people they knew; a few lucky children (mostly girls) could attend two of them, depending on their circumstances.

Saint Rafael's, one of the newer shelters, arranged their

own Fourth of July party and invited girls from the camp in Florida City. The eighty boys would be joined by eighty girls. Father Walsh lived there and would supervise activities for this large group in the courtyard.

The other all-male shelters did the same, so every Fourth of July party could be "co-ed." Even Florida City invited boys from several shelters, so the girls could socialize with young Cuban men. This was the first time all the shelters celebrated a national holiday. At every Fourth of July party, the Cuban and the American flags were flown.

"The idea came from the children," Father Walsh explained at the Catholic Welfare Bureau's post-event meeting. "They said they wanted to honor both countries, and we thought that was a good idea."

"And those young ladies in Florida City were flirting with their guests," remembered James Baker. Along with Father Walsh and other staff members, he had dropped in on as many parties as possible. The Pedro Pans were happy to have them there to share in the fun.

"Speaking of Florida City, Father Walsh, I recently met Mayor Navilio and he told me an incredible story," James said mildly.

"What was it?" asked Father Walsh.

"He said you had been friends for some time when you asked him about leasing a facility for girls and young boys. Apparently, in late 1961 you discovered some empty apartment buildings that he owned, and told him the Catholic Welfare Bureau would lease the apartment complex if he would add a dining room and fence. The arrangement would give your program much needed space, and improve his bottom line."

Father Walsh threw back his head and laughed. "Well,

that's certainly one way to describe our agreement. He's a good man and a true friend who was there when we needed him."

"And Florida City became your largest facility, correct?"

"Yes, James. Young ladies of all ages and boys up to twelve years old live there. I think the children are happy because it feels like a home atmosphere."

"What makes it different from other shelters that have so many problems?"

"Because Cuban couples are house parents. And the administrator is a Cuban cleric—Father Salvador de Cisterna."

Another Catholic Welfare Bureau board member raised his hand. "May I ask a question, Father Walsh?"

"Of course, please do," answered Father Walsh. "What's on your mind?"

"Can the young girls relate to a male administrator, when they need to feel a female touch and be fussed over? We know they need their mothers."

Father Walsh smiled reassuringly. "Ah, we are fortunate to have six Sisters of St. Philip Neri, who once ran private schools in Cuba. They love them and understand these children very well."

Another priest on the board added. "Don't forget we also have Cuban-American staff, who offer the same support there as at Matecumbe and Kendall. And all of them organize important outside social activities."

"Such as the wonderful weekend pastimes we've initiated in these shelters?" asked James Baker.

"Yes," answered the young priest. "I'm new here, but I've heard that picnics, trips to the beach and dances are encouraged to help maintain a semblance of normal social life in these abnormal circumstances." He glanced around to gage their reactions.

Father Walsh, thoughtful and attentive, took some time to answer. "We have set up tents for movies, Mass and performances put on by the children. Because of its unique setup this Florida City camp offers an opportunity for these young women to act as role models for the children."

"How is the education system working there?" another board member wondered.

"The older children attend local schools nearby in Homestead, while the younger ones have classes at the center."

"Are there any other questions before we call it a day?"

It seemed there were none. The meeting ended without further discourse.

On their way out, all eight board members stopped to thank Father Walsh. James Baker was the last to leave.

"Bryan, you are amazing! No matter what the world sees, the Lord appreciates your vision and sacrifices."

Father Walsh smiled. "Thank you, James."

James was suddenly serious. "I think the Lord has many more blessings in store for you."

Blessings? Father Walsh thought. *More blessings? I have abundant blessings in my life. I have a car that four boys fit into; with it I can drop my boys off at the movies and pick them up two hours later, or even take them sailing in a boat I can rent cheaply."*

Suddenly he remembered an article he had intended to share with James. "Did you see the *New York Times* article from May 27th?" he asked. "It describes our Pedro Pan program, and they call it 'the largest peacetime program for homeless children in this country.'"

James smiled. "Yes, Bryan. They also say we now have

ten thousand unaccompanied Cuban children in the States, with five hundred arriving each month."

Father Walsh was pensive. "Is it really so many? I believe they have exaggerated. We will have to check."

Yet he felt peaceful, knowing that he ran this unwieldy, dynamic program as efficiently as possible. His rules were humane, yet fairly enforced. The most serious violations of the regulations might result in a paddling, but only he was allowed to touch the children. (Boys could choose between a bamboo, wooden or leather paddle). Thankfully, this last resort had only been necessary a few times.

Consequences much more frequently enforced were losing part of their allowance or revoking permission to leave the camp during their free time.

All the boys agreed that Father Walsh was a great man— "Like a father to us." They also said that although he was strict about the rules, they felt they were treated fairly and protected. They were relieved that someone took a loving interest in their welfare and development. Another common observation was: "He is a man of great compassion."

His guiding principles were: to make the boys feel at home, to know we're happy they are here, and to love them. He strove to make them happy under difficult circumstances, while keeping the memory of their parents and their culture alive.

"I don't know how you do it, my friend. God bless you, as you've blessed them."

Father Walsh sat up straighter. "Just today I was asked the definition of contentment. I responded that it's always doing everything you possibly can and being satisfied, whatever the outcome. Each effort we make is its own reward."

James nodded thoughtfully. "And it's a feeling of calm that comes from inside. That's what *Operation Pedro Pan* has done for us. Right, Bryan?"

"Let us always remember to give ourselves permission to feel that sense of calm."

James was moved yet again by the depth of feeling in his friend's eyes.

23

August 19, 1962

Sunday Mass has become the pivotal link between our present and our past. As we sit and kneel and genuflect and listen to the Latin and participate in the rituals during Mass, we think longingly about being home, sharing these acts of faith with our parents in Cuba. Back then I never would have imagined that in a few years Agustín and I would be living far away from them, in a shelter in Miami.

How were they doing? What were they thinking about this morning as they attended Mass? The last moments together at the airport were our final hugs for who knows how long. There are those rushed three-minute phone calls every month, but how much can we share of ourselves and our feelings in three minutes? Letters are poor substitutes for parents. We need to feel their arms around us, Mamá's kisses on our cheeks, and Papá's arms around our shoulders. I'm worried that our parents will become just mental images, or even worse, a blurred vision. Absence does not make the heart grow fonder for children. It makes them feel abandoned.

Agustín asks me a lot of questions about why they sent us here without them. I answer him honestly, explaining that it was a very difficult decision for them to make, based on a sacrifice that we couldn't possibly understand. It makes so little sense to either of us. But we must have faith that it will someday. Life is full of twists and turns that end up having enormous consequences.

We had just changed our clothes to go outdoors when a nun met us at the doorway. "Phone call for you two from Cuba," she announced with a grin.

Agustín dashed to the infirmary's east wall to snatch up the dangling receiver. *"¿Aló? ¿Mamá, eres tú?* (Is that you, Mamá)?"

"Sí mi amor. (Yes, my love). Are you well? We haven't heard from you in several weeks."

I listened as Agustín assured her we were fine and yes, we had written them recently.

"We think our visas will be here any day now, so we can join you soon. Isn't that great news?" she exclaimed.

My brother nodded happily and gave me the phone. I answered for us both. "Yes, Mamá, it's wonderful news! Where is Papá?"

"He's in line getting our monthly ration." Then I remembered the *Supplies Booklet*, entitling each family to a certain amount of food and other basic necessities. If you missed your designated day, you'd get nothing for another month.

"Give him our love, Mamita. And best of luck in getting the visas and arriving here soon. Please keep us informed," I encouraged her before returning the phone to Agustín to say goodbye. Their news surprisingly troubled me and reminded me of how much I missed them and how different life was without them.

"Let's go play some baseball, little brother. Pray for Mamá and Papá."

I've had to learn to deal with my intense feelings. Every

time I think I've learned to accept my problems and live with them, I feel assaulted by unfamiliar emotions and challenges. Moving in with a foster family would mean being able to escape this place; but what could I do for those good and brave people who would take us in? Bringing everything together so everyone could be happy would be absolute proof of the existence of God, yet I have become more furious with the idea of God as each day passes without that happening.

If He did exist, why was He separating families, forcing so many to struggle in their own country? Why did He allow Fidel Castro to ruin Cuba? I realized what a heavy burden my parents were being forced to carry, yet they had chosen separation from us over repression. I ached for them physically and emotionally. If we ended up living with foster parents, I thought that would be like admitting that our parents were really gone. That was the ultimate betrayal in my turbulent mind.

A heavy feeling of deep despair settled over me like a smothering blanket. I finally understood that my parents, like those of thousands of other Cuban children, loved us so much they were willing to lose us in order to save us. Tears were pooling in my eyes.

That realization broke me. I pushed myself up from the table and ran from the tent, sprinting wildly toward the woods. Something exploded in my mind and I heard wrenching sobs racking my body. I shouted out that I did not deserve this freedom while my own country was dying. I threw myself to the ground, wailing and pounding the earth as I screamed about all the evil things I had thought and done. Finally collapsing, sapped of all energy, I heard the songbirds trying to console me. They had stayed with me and shared my grief.

Leonardo was the first boy we met the evening we arrived at Matecumbe. Now he was leaving for his foster home. I remembered him calling Matecumbe the *Infierno Verde* (Green Hell), and we had hopefully doubted his opinion. Now he would fly away to join a foster family in Colorado.

"Leonardo, you should be so happy to be escaping," I teased. "I hope you get a good *beca* and that your parents come for you soon."

He shook his head. "I'm not happy to leave. At least here I have friends, and I'm closer to Cuba. I'll be even further away now." He added, eyes downcast. "No one knows the future."

I understood his feelings. I couldn't imagine going on to *another new life* before I had made sense of the one I had been dropped into.

Señor George Guarch rounded up the four young men who were leaving: three brothers and Leonardo. We had become friends with them all, and I knew I would miss them.

Padre Palá walked to the car and spoke to them one last time. "Onward, *mis muchachos* (my boys). A new life awaits you. Good luck to each of you. *Vayan con Dios* (Go with God)."

"Write to us, guys," I yelled to them as the car pulled away.

Only Leonardo wrote to us. And his first letter was a complete shock.

24

September 20, 1962

These past three weeks have been tough and discouraging for Agustín and me. He found metal scraps in his breakfast oatmeal, which we thought was an accident. I took the bowl into the kitchen and asked if anyone new had worked the kitchen this morning.

"Yes, we've had several new boys working in here to make extra allowance, but they've been here for a while now. Why do you ask?"

I explained what happened and they apologized and said they would immediately look into it. My brother shrugged it off and said he thought it was an accident and not to worry about it.

Then I found tacks in my bunk bed, between the sheets. Fortunately, I felt them with my fingers before I laid down. I didn't want Agustín to know about it. The next morning I discovered one leg of my jeans shredded by knife slashes. Now I knew we were being bullied.

I confided in Alberto, and we agreed to keep whatever decisions we made between the two of us. We didn't want our younger brothers to be frightened or become accomplices in how we chose to resolve this.

Several days later we received a letter from Leonardo, which shook us to the core.

Dear Rodolfo and Agustín,

I have waited for a while before writing. I hoped that things would get better, but now I have to admit to you that I got a bad "beca." My foster parents are Cuban, but not like the Cubans we knew when we lived there or even those living in Miami. Their names are Señor and Señora Vidal, and that's what we call them. There are seven of us in this small house, and I am crowded in a small bedroom with three others.

We have many rules: make our beds, our breakfasts, and our lunches. Everybody wants to be the first to make breakfast, because it takes a while to toast the bread and make our sandwich. We make our sandwich with mayonnaise, nothing more. We have to rush to get to the school bus on time.

Señora Vidal makes dinner and we all eat at six o'clock. Afterwards, we boys wash the dishes and clean the kitchen. We are each assigned certain tasks that are rotated weekly.

On Saturday, we have to clean the whole house and both cars. We swap these chores according to her schedule. Then she inspects, and if one or more of us hasn't done a good job, we are grounded for the rest of the weekend.

Sunday we go to the laundromat and wash, dry and fold our clothes. They give us the coins for the machines and the soap. We get an allowance of seventy-five cents a week, and we can do what we want after the chores are finished. They don't pay for haircuts or health issues, including dentists or doctors. If you fight with another boy in the house, that's your problem and they won't interfere. If you cry or complain about anything, they tell you to shut up.

Three of the older boys here are thugs. They make rules for the rest of us to follow, and the Vidals don't say a thing. You can't have anything the thugs don't have, so the bicycle that my uncle bought for me disappeared. They sold it and kept the money. I told the Señora and she said I was a spoiled brat and that I didn't deserve anything the others didn't have.

I didn't fight back because they are bigger, and if I don't submit to their will, I will be hit or beaten up. They belong to a local gang and have their meetings on weekends at the McDonald's Restaurant. They steal switchblades and other items from the hardware stores, and have threatened us if we tell. They also steal food and magazines.

There are only three good things for me here. I like school, and it is my escape. We can go anywhere we want, anytime, after we finish our chores. There are no curfews but we have to be home for breakfast, dinner and when the school bus arrives. The third thing that is good is that my uncle lives about two hours away and has come to visit me twice. He explained that he can't foster me because his wife told him she doesn't want to.

I hope you are well and that your parents will come soon. Pray that mine will too, so I can get out of here. Please say hello to the others, and if you think it will help, let Padre Palá and Father Walsh read my letter. Maybe they can help me and the others here.

Sincerely,
Leonardo

Poor Leonardo. If only I could tell Father Walsh and he could do something for him.

Alberto and I were keeping our eyes and ears wide open, trying to sniff out clues and discover who the culprits were. We thought there had to be more than one, and we wanted to catch them in the act.

I woke up in the middle of the night hearing someone crying. It was Agustín, so I hopped down to his bed. "*¿Qué pasó, hermanito* (What happened, little brother)?" I whispered, reaching out to squeeze his hand. "Did you have a bad dream?"

He shook his head, sniffed and wiped his nose. "No, I had a beautiful dream about the Malecón in Havana. Remember when we went last year for a holiday?"

I did remember. It was the last holiday we spent with our parents, and we loved being in Havana.

"What do you remember about the Malecón, Agustín? Tell me your memories," I urged him.

He shifted on the bunk so I could sit with him. He was still sniffling, but not as much. "I remember the noise the waves made crashing against the wall. It was a different sound than where we lived; it was louder. And I remember the fortress of El Moro and the fun we had exploring that," he grinned. "What do you remember, Rodolfo?"

"The mile-long seawall (*El Malecón*) and all the couples making their daily *paseos* (promenades) hand in hand. How I'd love to take a new love in the future and show her the water," I said. "And the color of the water—just a little more mixture of turquoise and dark blue-green than we have in the eastern part of the island. Oh, and I can just visualize the waves throwing light spray high into the air, especially at sunset, when the sky explodes into strings of color: gold, blue, green and pink. So many shades of pink. We made up names for them, remember?"

Agustín was smiling now, as we tried to hold onto our precious memories. I wanted to give him more.

"Remember the ice cream vendors, and that thick delicious ice cream we bought from them? There was one on every corner. You asked Papá to buy two cones, just for you!" I said, laughing.

"And you wanted to fish off the seawall, so Mamá asked two teenagers to rent out their fishing rods so we could! That probably was an unexpected surprise for them," he remembered.

"I also miss our beach, covered with fine white sand that always got between our toes. I miss the skinny palm trees that waved in the sky above us," I added. "They say our beaches have the most beautiful clear water anywhere. Mamá used to tell us it was like crystal, with fish skimming the surface, showing off their colors as they darted through the waves."

Agustín's face grew solemn. "Do you think we'll ever see those waters again, Rodolfo?"

I sat up straighter and slowly shook my head. "I don't know. Maybe when Castro is gone and Cuba returns to normal. Maybe we'll all be there together. We can only hope."

"Thanks, Rodolfo," he murmured as he hugged me. "I'm going back to sleep now. See you tomorrow."

A few days later, as I climbed up onto my bed, it crashed down on the bottom bunk. Luckily, no one was underneath. Everyone rushed from the bathroom, the patio and everywhere else to see what had happened.

"Are you okay, Rodolfo?" screamed Agustín, eyes wild as he ran into my arms.

I nodded. I knew what had happened. We inspected the corners of the bunk and found the screws and brackets had been loosened enough to come apart when I lay on the mattress.

I sent one of the older boys to get Padre Palá. Shaking his head indignantly, he brought in the camp handyman to fix it. Then he took me outside.

"Has anything else been going on with you or your brother?" he asked.

I told him everything I could think of and showed him my jeans.

"We will resolve this quickly. In the meantime, be watchful and say nothing, not even to Agustín."

"Sí, Padre. Thank you. I hope you can find out who is doing this."

Three days later, two of the older boys who had laughed at the pool when I rescued the drowning Ramón were quietly taken away. Nobody from the staff would tell us where they had gone, but the rumor was that they were given a beating from Father Walsh, and then left Miami. We'll probably never know for sure who was behind it, but no more evil pranks were committed at Matecumbe for as long as we were there.

25

October 3, 1962

W as it just a coincidence, or heavenly intervention? About two weeks after Father Walsh had dealt with the two malicious older boys, Agustín and I were told Padre Palá wanted to see us in his office.

When we sat down, he told us we had received a *beca* to live in New York, at an orphanage called *Mission of the Immaculate Virgin, Mount Loretto* on Staten Island. I was devastated.

"What? No Sir! Padre Palá, please don't send us to an orphanage," I begged him. "Let us stay here until our parents come. They should be here any time now." I felt drained and dizzy.

"Rodolfo, several days ago your parents told you they did not yet have their visas. I spoke to them last night and explained the sudden opportunity you were given to go together to New York. They agreed that would be a positive move, especially since you two will stay together."

Agustín sat quietly in a folding chair, his head bent and tears streaming down his face. The priest moved another chair over and put an arm around his shoulders, saying reassuringly, "Agustín, this will be for the best. I promised your parents I wouldn't separate you, and I've found a way to keep that promise."

I felt furious and betrayed, but refused to raise my voice or fall apart. I rested my face in my hands to gather strength and stay calm. "When do we leave?"

"In two days." His expression softened. "But I do have some good news as well."

We waited for him to speak.

"Your friends Alberto and Sergio Ochoa will be joining you there. I hope this can make the move easier for all four of you."

Agustín wiped his eyes with the back of his hand. "Gracias a Dios. We'll have some friends even before we get there," he mumbled, half-heartedly.

The Manhattan skyline impressed us as we rode the Staten Island Ferry to the orphanage. The priest who had met us at the airport bought all four of us roast beef sandwiches for lunch, while warning us not to expect food this delicious where we were going.

The Mission of the Immaculate Virgin, Mount Loretto, sat on the far side of Staten Island. Pulling into the dock we saw the steeple first, then the rest of the Church of St. Joachim and St. Anne. The complex turned out to be very large; I read later in a brochure that it was three hundred seventy-five acres of rustic waterfront property.

Father Ogilvie, the priest who was giving us the tour, pointed to the cemetery in the distance. "Here lie some of the orphans who served in World War II. Father John Drumgoole, the founder of the orphanage, is also laid to rest here."

"How many children are housed here?" wondered Alberto.

"A little over nine hundred now, ages six to eighteen.

You boys will live on one side of the property and the girls on the other. It works out better that way."

Then he added, "This year we celebrate the orphanage's ninetieth birthday. Did they tell you this is the largest child-caring institution in the United States?"

I groaned and squeezed my brother's shoulder. He looked up at me, and I winked. "We'll be fine here, *hermanito.*"

After being taken to a bunk room in special living quarters away from the other boys, we asked why. "We'll be seeing them at meals and activities, so why not get to know them as soon as possible?" I asked.

When Father Ogilvie asked the management that question, we were moved to the main living area.

Father Ogilvie told us that boys our age went to a vocational school run by the orphanage, and we asked him if we could please go to a regular high school instead. We had gone to one in Miami and were hoping to go to college and have professional careers someday. I was amazed at how easy it was to persuade them—they not only listened to us but agreed to our requests. Maybe this place wouldn't be so bad after all.

So the next week we signed up at Tottenville High School on Staten Island and were pleased to learn we would be in some of the same classes.

And in their grade, Agustín and Sergio would be together in all but one class.

Many of the rules we had here were the same as in Matecumbe, along with an annoying new one: roll calls. When they called out your name, you had to stand against a wall and announce forcefully, "Present." If you weren't there, you would be scolded the first time and then lose your Saturday permission to leave the grounds.

Every Saturday, after we had finished mopping and buffing floors, washing dishes, helping with the yard work, etc., we were allowed to go where we wanted between 11:00 a.m. and 4:00 p.m. But everyone had to be back before 4:00 p.m.—no exceptions.

Our counselors and the priests in charge enforced this rule like military officers. I decided they were being harder on the growing number of Cubans so the others wouldn't think we had preferential treatment.

One morning at breakfast, a framed article from the local newspaper appeared on the dining room wall. After our morning prayer, the priest suggested we all read it. The article was from the *Staten Island Advance*, written on September 6, 1962.

Against the changing tides of the child welfare system, the Mission of the Immaculate Virgin, Mount Loretto, *is a rock. The immigrant orphans who once milled about The Mount now adorn the walls of the church's photo gallery. The blind girls are gone, the waves of refugee children from revolutionary Cuba and war-torn Vietnam have ebbed. Today their beds are occupied by the developmentally and emotionally disabled, mostly black, many the victims of poverty, drugs, abuse and neglect.*

None of us understood why we were asked to read this. It wasn't even totally factual, because there are only a few disabled people, and we refugee children are still living here.

We had some minor run-ins with the boys who were undeniably hardened by life: not orphans, but not wanted by their parents, or running away from broken homes. As Cuban kids, we were not used to fighting or being bullied, and in Cuba some of our friends were black or mixed so color meant nothing to us. But here we could see the pecking order. Once the thugs realized we were not interested in them and we had nothing they wanted, they pretty much left us alone.

"Hey, today I saw a younger teenager with a book titled *The Rise and Fall of the Third Reich* tucked under his arm. The cover was black with a white swastika. I asked him why he carried it," Alberto told us.

"Did he tell you?" asked Sergio, unfamiliar with the title.

"Yeah, it was real strange. He said the resident hoodlums here are afraid of crazy people because they are so unpredictable. The book was part of his survival plan."

Alberto paused for a few seconds. "The guy told me, 'With this book under my arm and the crazy eyes I sometimes make walking around, they stay away from me.' I told him we'd try it if we needed to, and he laughed."

"Is he Puerto Rican?" I asked. "I think I've seen him in the bunk room without the book and he told me he's from San Juan."

Other Cuban refugees and some other Hispanic boys were becoming more evident in the main living areas.

One day the director of the orphanage took us aside. "You boys have made a real difference here. Following your suggestion to put all the boys together in one living area has increased interactions among all of you. And you might have noticed that we've started letting older boys attend the public high school if they don't want a vocational career."

When he shook our hands and walked away, we felt surprised and pleased. Maybe this *beca* wasn't so bad after all? The food was about the same as we had at Matecumbe, and the rules very similar. So far we've kept our distance from problems and spend our free time together.

We don't feel the need to make other friends here. But school is the best reward. It's a real good deal, because there are nice teachers and some very pretty girls in our classes.

26

October 10, 1962

Her name is Maureen, but everyone calls her Mimi. She's in two of my high school classes and has quickly become a very important person in my life.

I felt shy my first day in high school. I knew only three people, including my brother. My English is not great and I have a heavy Spanish accent, but I understand everyone and am usually understood.

Then this pretty girl walked over to me the first week in homeroom. "Are you new here? I haven't seen you before. My name is Mimi."

Her bright blue eyes were warm, confident and poised.

"Yes, I am new. I'm only staying at *Mount Loretto* until my parents arrive from Cuba."

She frowned. "Why aren't they here with you?"

I told her the story of the exodus of the Cuban children. She listened, riveted. When I finished, she said softly, "I'm so sorry you and Agustín have been separated from them for so long. I will pray they can come here soon." After a moment, she added "I think your accent is very pleasant."

We quickly became friends and have already spent two Saturdays together in Tottenville, sharing an early movie and lunch. She always pays for her movie ticket and meal, probably realizing that I don't have much money.

I told her about an idea one of the nuns had given me to earn extra money. Father Kehan, who is kind to the boys from other countries, offered to help us look for after-school jobs.

"I hope to start working soon and save some money to help with my parents' airline tickets. But I'll also use some of the money when I go into town on Saturdays."

"That sounds wonderful, Rodolfo." Mimi had cute dimples on either side of her encouraging smile.

"Meanwhile," she said, why not come to my house for lunch next Saturday? I could pick you up and get you back to *Mount Loretto* on time."

I gladly accepted, and could think of nothing else for the rest of the week.

Alberto met a friend of Mimi's named Suzi and is now "dating" her. He had an interesting experience with her right after they got together.

Last Saturday, after he and Suzi had gone to the movies, Alberto missed the 4:00 p.m. *Mount Loretto* curfew. Sergio became worried and came looking for me.

"What do we do now, Rodolfo?" he asked in a panic.

"I'm sure he'll have a good reason for being late," I told him. We waited together with Agustín, playing card games to distract ourselves. Two hours later, Alberto limped through the front gate with a policeman and was confronted by the nasty head counselor, Mr. Furlong.

We found him the following morning, asleep in his bunk.

After Mass he told us what had happened. "Suzi and I went to the movies and then to her bus stop. We'd missed her 3:30 p.m. bus and waited together on the bench for the next one, talking, holding hands, and sharing a kiss or two as other buses went by." He looked embarrassed.

"Her bus didn't come until almost 5:00 p.m. I said good-bye and started running back to the orphanage, knowing I'd be in trouble. It was so far I didn't get back until almost 6:00 p.m."

His expression changed from embarrassment to anger. "Mr. Furlong grabbed me by my coat collar, yanked me up in the air and slapped me hard across the face. His glove strap left a mark. Can you still see it? Then, in front of the policeman, he screamed at me that I was only a Cuban refugee and that if I broke another rule, he would put me out on the street." There was a flash of fire in his eyes.

Bile rose in my throat and I could hardly breathe.

"The police officer asked me if I had run away and I told him 'no,' which infuriated Mr. Furlong—he must have hoped I'd be quiet and taken down to the police station. Thank God the officer believed me and refused."

"Then Mr. Furlong took me out to a fenced yard in back and ordered me to stand with my arms up straight over my head for three hours. It was cold, I had no hat on and my ears burned painfully from the freezing wind."

"Then you came to bed, right?" asked Sergio. "Why didn't you wake me up to tell me you were back?"

"I was too tired to talk, and you were all asleep." He obviously felt humiliated.

"When he let me back inside he sneered: 'I'm taking away your weekly allowance for the next six weeks. Guess you won't be able to write your parents, or go to the movies.'"

I couldn't accept that and quickly retorted. "Yes you will, Alberto. From next Sunday on, we will all have part-time jobs. Just between us, I guarantee you'll have your stamp money and you can keep writing your family."

Father Kehan kept his word, and we each made $2.50

washing the bedding, folding sheets and towels, taking out garbage cans for pick-up, washing dishes, and sweeping out the storage buildings. That was more money than we'd seen at one time since our arrival. This small sacrifice of a few free evening hours brought us countless benefits.

Months later we learned that the money we earned from Father Kehan had come from his own pocket.

Mimi and I spent many of our school lunch periods together after that, packing our own lunch boxes so we could eat in one of the cafeteria's back rooms. Agustín and Sergio were such good friends that my brother didn't mind eating with his classmates. Alberto often ate lunch with Suzi.

Mimi is so lovely. She has long silky dark hair, dimples that brighten her smile, sparkling blue eyes, and a tall athletic body. She plays basketball on the high school girls' team and is eagerly looking forward to every practice and the games that will start soon.

One day she told me that she liked my hair—light brown, wavy and worn a little longer than most because I didn't like the crew cuts the orphanage barbers gave us. She also said my dark brown eyes contrasted with my hair, which made for an interesting package. Her way with words always makes me feel special.

"Rodolfo, if you want, the next time you come to my house for lunch, my older sister can cut your hair. She's going to beauty school and loves to cut hair, and is really quite good at it."

So the following Saturday her sister cut my hair. It looked much better, and her whole family admired my new style. Then Mimi and I sat in front of the fireplace in her cozy library, where she asked me about life in Cuba.

"Well, you know I'm from Santiago de Cuba, the second largest city on my island. It's on a bay connected to the Caribbean Sea, and it's a really beautiful place. I miss it a lot. I'd love to show it to you one day."

"Tell me more. What did you do growing up?"

"We swam every day during the summer, and almost every weekend during the rest of the year. The ocean is so clear and calm, with small turquoise waves; there are coral reefs not far offshore. And in our back yard are guava, mamey, orange, and papaya trees; we had it all. We especially loved climbing up our favorite tree: the great mango. We went out on the branches and knocked delicious fruit to the ground, using sticks or our own fists." She seemed almost as excited about the memories as I was.

"Oh Rodolfo, I hope to discover Cuba, meet your parents, and experience all these things with you some day."

I suddenly felt like telling her something I thought about everyday living here on Staten Island. "Mimi, living at the orphanage reminds me of an orphanage we had in my home town, *El Asilo Padre Francisco*, named after the priest who had founded it many years ago. I never paid much attention to it growing up, but when I return to Cuba, I want to help them out in any way I can."

Mimi took my hand in hers. "I know you will, and I'm very proud of you."

Mimi brought me a feeling I hadn't experienced since leaving Cuba: comfort. I was so grateful for that. Maybe I was falling in love?

27

October 17, 1962

Father Walsh's very busy daily routine had to be put aside over the past several days. He had to digest a series of announcements and political statements that threatened to put the entire project, and many people connected to it, in danger.

And he knew that millions of American lives were also in danger.

The threat of nuclear war wasn't something he could do anything about. But he felt personally responsible for the well-being of the *Operation Pedro Pan* children and their parents. Recognizing the extreme stress and anxiety that recent news stories would cause, he also knew his group's response should be guided by careful reflection and collaboration.

So he called an emergency meeting of his staff, along with several military consultants who had advised him in the past. He also invited the priests in charge of the shelters.

"Good evening, my friends. And thank you for coming on such short notice. We are here tonight to share intelligence and discuss possible solutions to a very relevant crisis," he began. "Please listen to my report before asking questions. I'll be happy to answer them all shortly." He smiled appreciatively.

James Baker watched him closely, aware of what he was about to reveal.

"Most of you heard President Kennedy's televised radio speech two nights ago. I have a copy of it here, which I will read to you. *'It shall be the policy of this nation to regard any nuclear missile launched from Cuba against any nation in the Western hemisphere as an attack on the United States, requiring a full retaliatory response upon the Soviet Union.'*"

He took a sip of water before giving the group more details behind the president's shocking announcement.

"On October 14th, American U-2 spy planes flying reconnaissance missions over Cuba took pictures of four long-range Soviet missiles in Cuba. They're capable of reaching any point in the continental United States within a few minutes of being launched, and their nuclear warheads would cause mass destruction. President Kennedy had warned Soviet leader Nikita Khrushchev that there would be grave consequences if the Soviet Union were to install offensive weapons in Cuba, but now it is clear that Khrushchev hasn't taken the threat seriously."

He paused a moment to let the ramifications sink in. "The United States has already installed several nuclear sites in Turkey and Italy with the range to strike Moscow. The President is responding to evidence that Cuba is not only a strategic outpost for the spread of communism in the Americas, but also about to become the base from which the Soviet nuclear weapons could reach New York, Chicago and Washington almost instantaneously."

You could have heard a pin drop in the room. This was earth-shattering, and the burden was overwhelming for *Operation Pedro Pan's* participants and leaders.

One of the priests glanced out the window as if expecting to see an incoming missile.

"Tensions will become intense here. As the children's guardians and mentors, we must be prepared to handle their questions, and show them our commitment to reuniting them with their parents even as their world seems to be spinning out of control."

All eyes were on Father Walsh. He ended his anxious overview with an unexpected analogy. "Life should be peaceful sometimes. It should be a whisper and not always a scream. But we must deal with what we've been given. I do pray for each one of you to have the understanding that it is our duty to love on and guide these children, under all circumstances."

He began to sit down, but then remembered to ask for questions.

"Yes, Father Walsh," one of the priests began. "The children will learn about this development soon, and naturally be frightened—terrified that they or their parents may be blown up. Should we allow them to watch the news?" asked one of the priests.

"Yes, let them watch. Watch it in groups with an adult leader who can try to answer their questions. Some will want to phone their parents, and I'm sure you will do everything possible to help them do that."

The Army general offered a comment. "Father Walsh, let your priests and camp leaders know that covert operations of *Operation Mongoose* are under way as we speak. That should make everyone feel a little better."

"Thank you, General. I will give your contact information to everyone in this group so they can reassure themselves and the people they're working with."

"Father Walsh, should we mention the possibility of

nuclear war?" another priest asked. "And should we ask psychiatrists or counselors available to help children deal with the chaos and stress?"

Father Walsh understood his colleague's concern. "Father Villanueva, I would say no to both questions at this time. Let's monitor what unfolds in the next few days."

Father Palá raised his hand. "The shelters could also bring in leaders of the *Juventud Estudiantíl Católica* (Student Catholic Youth) to share a more positive perspective with the children. I will be happy to help with that."

"Thank you, Father Palá."

James Baker had a question. "I wonder what will happen to those parents who already hold visas to come to Miami. Do you have any idea?"

"James, I cannot answer that, but I can report that I receive over four thousand visa requests per week. You may know that William Vanden Heuvel, president of the *International Rescue Committee*, recently testified to Congress that 'the reunion of separated families is the basic attribute of any normalization of family life.' And also, the State Department has begun issuing visa waivers to entire families in an attempt to curtail the number of unaccompanied children under the care of the government."

That surprised most people sitting at the conference table.

"Father Walsh, since the beginning of *Operation Pedro Pan*, how many children have made it to the United States?" The question was asked by Father Salvador De Cistierna from the Florida City shelter.

"Over fourteen thousand, Father De Cistierna. I can't say off the top of my head, but on March 9th, *The New York Times* wrote that there were 14,072. Our count is about 14,048."

After everyone but James Baker had left, Father Bryan Walsh prayed out loud. "Heavenly Father, have mercy on the decision makers of the USSR, the United States, and Cuba. Soften their hearts and guide them to reach the right solution. Be with the children and their separated parents; keep them hopeful and allow them to reunite one day soon. We thank You in advance for Your bountiful blessings. In Your precious name, Amen."

"Amen," whispered James. "Good night, Bryan. I'll see you tomorrow."

28

October 22, 1962

We gathered around the television to listen to President Kennedy's national address. He announced that in the face of the Soviet deployment of nuclear weapons in Cuba, he was ordering a total quarantine of the island and cancellation of all flights into and out of Cuba. He encouraged countries friendly to the United States to do the same thing.

For everyone connected to the Pedro Pan project, it was a heartbreaking and terrifying moment.

After a stunned silence, Agustín reacted as if he had just awakened from the worst nightmare of his life.

"Oh no," cried out Agustín, his voice trembling. "*Malísimas noticias*, Rodolfo. (Very bad news). Now Mamá and Papá can't come here in November!" When he gripped my arm, I could feel him shaking.

My throat closed up. When I did manage to speak, my voice cracked. "It's horrible news for us, Agustín, and for all those whose parents aren't here yet. But we can't lose hope and fall apart. Let's encourage them to find another way out." Even I could hear the anguish in my voice, which was stronger than my anger. But Cubans have always been known as creative survivors. We had never needed to be stronger for our families, and more determined to find solutions.

Four days earlier our parents had phoned us with their long-awaited news. They were holding visas in their hands and were approved for a departure in mid-November. The tickets could not be purchased until the exact date was set, but we had been thrilled to learn they were coming.

Now all our hopes seemed to have been dashed.

"Maybe it's just temporary and will change soon. Nobody knows what the next step will be," I said, trying to comfort both of us. Alberto and Sergio listened in anxious silence. They hadn't heard from their parents for over a month.

During the school hours, we attended classes as usual. The teachers tried not to discuss what the very real possibility of a nuclear war could mean. When I asked my math teacher what he thought, he shook his head and said everything was still in limbo. I told him that we Pedro Pan children were afraid that Cuba would be bombed and our parents would be killed. His sympathy and concern weren't enough. I urgently needed to get an explanation from someone who understood.

Padre Palá seemed surprised to get my telephone call, but quickly lifted my spirits.

"I have great news for you and the other three boys. In fact, I was about to send out this wonderful news in a packet with a new journal I want to mail you." His joy was infectious.

"What's going on, Padre Palá?"

"Our beloved friend, Father Walsh, was named *Monsignori* by the Pope on October 5th. I found out from James Baker's memo only a few days ago. Monsignor Walsh will be invested on December 21st! What an incredible honor, and how well-deserved it is!"

"That's so amazing for him, and also for *Operation Pedro Pan!*" I was truly happy for Father Walsh and excited to share this news with the others. "Could you please send us something about this in the mail so we can make copies for our families?"

"Indeed I shall, son. And one of his achievements for which he is being honored was the organization and coordination of *Operation Pedro Pan:* the Cuban children's program of care."

Then he changed the subject. "Rodolfo, I imagine you called about something weighing heavy on your heart. How can I help?"

I told him my concerns and all of our fears about Cuba's future and our prospects.

"Rodolfo, I understand how you must feel. Father Walsh is urging us to develop a nonviolent response to this ongoing tragedy. He has just published a journal called *Mensaje* (The Message) for our instructors in the shelters, which includes ways to organize and respond nonviolently. I'll send you copies of this along with information about Monsignor Walsh's appointment."

"Thank you so much, Padre Palá. But we need to explain to our parents about their chances of leaving Cuba, and if we can still keep in touch. Can you help with that?"

"Of course I shall, young man. Remember that God sometimes wounds us in order to save us. Tell them that, and don't let your faith waver."

Now we could only watch and wait.

October 28, 1962

There were many sleepless nights after watching the nightly news. The four of us worked together four days a week, and we discussed the still evolving missile crisis. Over the next several days, the disaster intensified. We listened to television reports, people who knew the updates, and even discussed the advice from Padre Palá in his letter. We knew President Kennedy called daily meetings with his security advisors. Diplomacy had already been taken off the table, but should the United States attack/invade Cuba?

The Joint Chiefs of Staff voted to invade, but the president was worried that this would lead to World War III between the U.S. and the Soviet Union. Then President Kennedy set up a naval blockade.

The Soviet Union refused publicly to back down. Yet Father Kehan heard there were secret negotiations between the two superpowers.

Agustín was beside himself with worry. "Rodolfo, do you think our parents will be killed instantly when the bombs explode?" he asked, tears filling his eyes. "And if we survive over here, will that make us actual orphans? Will we be adopted and separated? We won't have a country to return to, so will we become Americans?"

Poor Agustín. Poor Cuba and all the Pedro Pans. Had the whole world gone crazy in the four years since Castro marched victorious through our homeland?

Unexpectedly, hope returned. On October 27th, President Kennedy announced that the Soviets had agreed to remove nuclear weapons from Cuba in return for the

United States' promise to dismantle missiles in Turkey aimed at the Soviet Union. The United States also agreed not to invade Fidel Castro's Cuba, or support an invasion led by any other nation.

From the television news, we saw and heard that the world rejoiced. We at the orphanage cried tears of joy and relief, thrilled that our parents would survive and we would have our Cuba intact to return to one day.

Some Americans felt betrayed by President John Kennedy. They felt that he had sold out Cuba's people to end the crisis. They feared that, without the threat of U.S. invasion, Fidel and his regime would reign terror and the communists' hold on power could not be broken.

My parents were inconsolable. Amazingly, they were able to get a call through that evening.

My father spoke first. *"Ay, mis queridos hijos, ya no hay esperanza para nosotros."* (Ay, my dear sons, now there's no longer hope for us). Nothing will prevent Fidel from destroying the lives of the people he vowed to make free. We are shattered."

I was stunned into silence by his despair. "Why do you say that, Papá?" I moaned through tears.

"Don't you see, my son? President Kennedy was our final hope to bring Castro down and allow millions of Cubans to return home and rebuild their lives. I will not be able to hold on to my business, nor can I now bring my sons back home to live. Our life in Cuba is over."

He wept softly. My heart broke for him.

Mamá was too distraught to speak more than one hopeful sentence. "We will come to live with you in November, and together we will find a way."

Unfortunately, that wasn't to be.

29

November 10, 1962

Autumn is here—the season of Thanksgiving. Today our English teacher gave us a pre-holiday assignment: to write an essay about something we can be thankful for. I struggled a little, and then asked Mr. Parker after class if I could write about my country.

"Mr. Parker, my early years in Cuba were painful in some ways, yet beautiful at the same time. I want to write about a life that my classmates would find hard to imagine. It begins with how Fidel Castro came into power and what he has done to Cuba. Will that be okay?"

"Of course, Rodolfo," Mr. Parker replied kindly. "It's a story that could only be shared by someone who experienced it, and might help you deal with what must have been very traumatic."

It took me a little more than two weeks of research and writing to tell this complicated story. At the same time, I was busy with classes, working after school, trying to rest a little on the weekends, and finding time to write in between.

I tried to explain to Mimi why we wouldn't be seeing as much of each other for a while. She was as supportive as I'd hoped she would be.

"Don't worry about our Saturdays together, Rodolfo. I

know how meaningful this part of your life was, and reading it will help me to understand you more through your pain and sacrifice. We'll have a special date after you finish."

It was not easy to write. I remembered a lot of it, but had to ask my brother and my two Cuban friends to help me to sort it all out. I called Father Walsh and James Baker to guide me with important dates and details in Cuba's recent history. Father Kehan corrected my writing errors so the story would be easier to read. I had written it first in Spanish and we translated it together, but still there were some mistakes.

This was very important for me to write. After all, this is the ongoing story of so many families in Cuba.

When I was fifteen years old, in January 1959, I met Fidel Castro. He was standing on a tank that stopped in front of my grandfather's medical clinic in Camaguey during his victory march through Cuba. People were excitedly filling the sidewalks to see him. His tank stopped directly in front of my family. Fidel was waving, smiling, and kissing babies when my father nudged me forward to shake his hand. Fidel took it into his large sun-tanned hand and gave me a broad smile. This personal attention made me feel special.

Everyone in Cuba was excited to welcome this new leader and his promise of democracy. We had been thrilled to witness the overthrow of Batista's corrupt regime by an unknown twenty-six-year-old lawyer named Fidel Castro and his ragtag militia of poor farmers and desperate young men. Across the country, people were scribbling graffiti on walls: "Viva Fidel" and "Fidel Sí, Batista No."

Our parents and their friends were cheering the new

revolutionary movement, and everyone talked about Castro's military successes. Radio Rebelde gave full reports of every victory over the ruthless and brutal Batista—the leader who had exploited his citizens for purely personal gain. Many people wanted to believe Castro's promise of a brighter future for our nation.

When Castro's army, led by Comandante Che Guevara, captured the train Batista had sent to Santa Clara to resupply his troops, we all cheered. Then our own city—Santiago de Cuba—fell, and Batista watched many of his own soldiers deserting. He could see the writing on the wall: Castro would soon take over the country.

Batista had been planning his departure and had a fortune in gold and U.S. dollars waiting for him in Spain. At a party he hosted on New Year's Eve 1958, he cheerfully informed the room full of friendly rich and influential guests that he was leaving for Spain the next morning, by way of the Dominican Republic.

Fidel Castro assumed power the next day. Everyone in Cuba gleefully celebrated his welcome triumph. After seizing control of Havana and all government facilities, he began a national victory march, intended to rival one of Caesar's marches into Rome. He delivered speeches about the democratic system he would install, and how Cuba would prosper under his leadership. After Batista's cruel and despotic regime, most Cubans were eager to believe everything he promised.

Castro announced that Manuel Urrutia would be the country's interim president, and José Miró Cardoña would be the prime minister. He would humbly continue to serve as commander-in-chief of the armed forces. To emphasize his status, he always appeared in public in drab army fatigues. His brother Raúl, Che Guevara and other advisors also dressed like guerilla soldiers: their hair and beards long and unkempt, rifles over their shoulders to show citizens that after an era of sacrifice and struggles, Cuba was now "free."

In long patriotic speeches on endless television broadcasts, Fidel carefully promoted his image of a versatile young leader, hoping to make true believers of the lower classes. He even pitched for a baseball team of revolutionary soldiers. But my father and his friends were not convinced and wondered among themselves about the new leader.

Castro gradually began removing anyone he feared might mount a counter-revolution, using the same brutal methods that Batista had used against his enemies.

The cry "¡Paredón!" (To the Wall!) *soon became a rallying cry in every Cuban city. Che Guevara, Castro's chief prosecutor, detained and convicted hundreds of policemen and soldiers from Batista's regime to be tried for war crimes and human rights abuses. At first the executions only targeted former members of Batista's regime, but later extended to anyone who criticized Fidel's new government. Soon these executions were even being broadcast on national television.*

The regime used imprisonment, torture, and exile to stop dissent. Eleven-year-old Agustín and I knew how bad things were getting across the country, from adult conversations about how people around the world had begun criticizing Cuba's new regime. During a visit to the United States in April, Fidel reassured Americans in newspaper articles that his regime was not and never would be communist. President Dwight Eisenhower, already suspicious, refused to meet with him, and sent Vice-President Nixon to a meeting in his place.

It was becoming obvious that Fidel Castro was taking complete control of the country by any means necessary. He censored the press, banned free speech and limited religious freedom.

Six months after taking control, he announced a new "Agrarian Reform" program, under which all sugar plantations would be confiscated by the government, and their lands divided among the plantation's thousands of workers. This announcement was made in Havana to a huge audience of almost a million farmers, invited and bused to Havana to applaud his revolutionary program.

Most people escaping Cuba during the early 1960s were middle-class and upper-class Cubans whose skills would have been crucial in nation building. The Castro regime, recognizing that this "brain drain" could bring about Castro's downfall, limited the number of people allowed to leave. "Operation Pedro Pan" became an even more important way for Cubans to immigrate for freedom to the United States.

My father and his friends were increasingly concerned that Fidel would nationalize businesses and private properties. My father's clothing business was still operating, and he hoped it could continue. Yet he saw Castro's sugar plantation seizures as part of an alarming trend.

"Fidel even seized his own father's plantation and gave it to the workers," he told us. "Cuba's thriving free-market economy is being destroyed to support communist dogma."

As the new plan was being implemented nationally, hundreds of thousands of Cuban families finally realized that this beloved country was no longer theirs. Anyone who opposed the regime's changes faced brutal punishment. Even former Castro supporters might be shot or "disappeared."

When my father's friend—and early Castro supporter—Hugo Matos resigned from the government, the regime called him a traitor to the revolution and arrested him. He was found guilty of treason in December and sentenced to twenty years in prison. By the first anniversary of the triumph of the revolution, only nine of the twenty-one members of Castro's government remained in office.

Business and private sector communities were outraged. The prime minister resigned, followed by the man Castro had named president. Fidel Castro named himself the new prime minister and did not replace the president. Openly demonstrating his true goals for Cuba, Fidel formed a pact with the Soviet Union. Nikita Khrushchev had agreed to buy five million tons of Cuban sugar and supply us with oil, grain, and credit.

Civil unrest filled the streets in towns and cities. On January 25th of 1962, the Organization of American States expelled Cuba. Thirteen Latin American countries had already broken diplomatic relations with them.

Every day we heard shots fired and eventually people we knew were among those killed. Uniformed soldiers roamed the rooftops of homes and businesses, looking for "traitors and dissidents." Fidel finally proclaimed himself a "Marxist-Leninist and would be until the day he died." Everyone we knew was now alarmed.

People openly discussed leaving Cuba after Castro's announcement that everyone in the nation would have to serve in the military to "defend our nation from the Imperialist Yankees to the north." On February 3rd, President John F. Kennedy ordered a total embargo on Cuban imports, except for pharmaceuticals, depriving the Cuban government of approximately $25 million in annual revenues. The president of the United States said that the ban would reduce Cuba's ability to engage in acts of aggression and subversion against other countries.

Papá told everyone he knew they had to fight to keep their properties and businesses. We were all frightened. Going to school, where the priests, nuns, and other teachers were increasingly uncertain of their future positions, was so difficult for us. We even felt unsafe in our homes, because soldiers regularly came to question our parents.

An urgent alarm was sounded across Cuba when Fidel closed every public and private school in the country to begin his comprehensive educational reform, which included sending one thousand students to Russia. Then he converted several military posts into indoctrination centers, dedicated to eradicating illiteracy. Thousands of young people were relocated to the countryside to teach the peasants how to read.

Next on his agenda was "Patria Potestad"—his new plan for the government to remove children from their homes and educate them in the revolution's principles. My mother actually got a copy of this plan and wept as she read it.

"How can they take over the education of our children and brainwash them like this?" she asked desperately,

covering one hand with the other over her heart and breathing deeply. This revolution that she and Papá had once supported had become a nightmare.

Because of the embargo, food was in short supply. Mamá waited in long lines in the hope of buying vegetables or meat. Despite the fruit trees in our garden, we were often hungry. Fidel blamed the American embargo for the scarcity of food, soap and toilet paper. But even his new alliance with Russia didn't improve anything. I heard my parents arguing and Mamá crying many nights when they thought I was asleep. Mamá begged my father to take us and go to Spain or Miami before it became impossible. He held out, still hoping for change.

American and other foreign businesses were nationalized. Many former allies now stopped sending direct economic aid. Countless businesses had to shut down or lay off employees; thousands of people lost their incomes. The government was too financially strapped to help anyone.

Schools were closed and the teachers, priests and nuns lost their jobs. We helped them pack books and mementos into boxes before tearfully saying goodbye. We never returned to school in Cuba. Instead, we accompanied our parents to their jobs or just stayed home.

About this time Fidel declared that all Cubans would be economic equals. The currency lost its value; stocks, bonds, and saving accounts became worthless. Every Cuban received a one-time payment of two hundred new Cuban pesos. Business owners like my parents lost everything they'd worked so hard for. Many families buried jewels and currency in secret places around their yards.

Now everyone knew Fidel was insane, and that life as they knew it in Cuba was over. Many professionals and business class people went into self-imposed exile. Thousands of Cuban families were torn apart, and Agustín and I missed seeing most of our cousins and many friends. We felt abandoned and very sad to see everyone leaving us.

Then in April of 1961 there was even more bad news. Fifteen hundred counter-revolutionary Cuban exiles, who'd been training in Central America and backed by the CIA, came ashore at the Bahia de Cochinos (the Bay of Pigs) on April 17th. They were hoping to win the support of the Cuban citizens, move on to Havana, and forcefully remove Castro from power.

President Kennedy authorized this program, which ended in devastating failure. Fidel's Air Force sank two of the invaders' ships. The soldiers were left stranded on beaches, without any backup. President Kennedy had to call off planned U.S. air strikes, to avoid the risk of war with the Soviet Union.

Ninety invading exiles had been killed, and one thousand two hundred were captured, tried and sentenced to prison for treason. Less than forty-eight hours later, Fidel addressed the nation declaring victory. The failure of the Yankee invasion was celebrated throughout the island as proof of Castro's military genius.

The trials were televised live daily. Our parents allowed us to watch one time in complete silence, and kept the television off after that. We were in mourning now for our country.

Agustín and I accompanied Mamá to Mass as always—our refuge from suffering and a source of hope.

As communism progressed, and the priests became increasingly vocal in their opposition, Fidel demanded that all priests and nuns, except the handful who openly supported him, leave the country at once.

Churches were closed and ransacked. Outraged citizens were powerless to do anything about it. We returned to visit our church—La Iglesia de las Mercedes—and sadly grieved over the damage. Hoodlums had broken, pulled down and demolished statues, stained-glass windows, and hand-carved doors. Golden chalices and candlesticks were looted, and every wall was disfigured by appalling graffiti messages. Human waste defaced the floors. It looked like every cross was defiled. The regime tried to blame this on the ousted priests, but everyone knew it was done under Castro's direction. Even at age seventeen, I was shocked to realize that no one would ever pray or say Mass there again.

Was Christ still here? I wondered aloud. Mamá said she thought He had left our country.

The growing loss of freedom, fear of persecution and the threat of losing their children to the communist government forced my parents to reach an unimaginable decision: to send their children away to the United States in order to save them.

I am forever grateful and thankful that they loved us enough to make this ultimate sacrifice.

30

November 23, 1962

Being away from our family without knowing when we would see them again might have made our first American Thanksgiving a very sad day. But it turned out to be wonderful, thanks to Mimi.

We had a four-day-weekend because Thursday was Thanksgiving. So Agustín and I eagerly accepted Mimi's invitation to join her and her family for the day. She assured us there would be many teenagers, since their relatives all gathered at her house for Thanksgiving dinner.

Alberto's girlfriend, Suzi, invited him and Sergio to her grandmother's home in New York City. All four of us would be able to learn more about this very American holiday. Some kids from the orphanage joined local families near the orphanage; others went to visit their family members. A festive Thanksgiving dinner was prepared at the orphanage for the children who stayed.

Our school classmates had already learned about the deeper meaning of Thanksgiving. So Agustín and I looked up the history on our own, and learned a lot about an important milestone in America's history, and the source of its patriotic spirit.

Sergio asked an interesting question after our research was complete. "There were no Pilgrims in Cuba, right?"

I shrugged. "Well, the people who came from other countries to mix in with those already living in Cuba were like the Pilgrims. But Cuba's history is very different from America's."

Our study and comparison of two very different countries helped us see the importance of learning more about one's home country's history, wherever it might be. And now that we're here, we realize how much we have to be thankful for.

As we were waiting for the meal to be served, two of Mimi's cousins asked if we could dance the Salsa. Penelope had heard some very danceable music coming from a Chinese Cuban restaurant in New York City, but had never seen anyone dancing it.

"I'm no expert, but we can show you some dance steps we used to do at our neighborhood fiestas," I told her. "But we don't have any instruments."

As usual, Agustín had a solution. He ran over to a table with drinks, picked up two empty aluminum soda cans, and beat them together to make a familiar Salsa beat, as if they were *clave* sticks.

Then I showed the two teenagers the basic Salsa steps: "Uno dos tres . . . cuatro cinco seis" and they quickly picked it up. Penelope's dad moved some living room furniture around to make a small dance floor . . . and soon half the teenagers and most adults were dancing with happy faces. Some of the parents danced the Cha-Cha—another native Cuban dance—along with the music. I remember my parents dancing that along with the Danzón, Cuba's official dance.

I think Agustín (our one-man *orquestra*) was having the most fun. Leading the impromptu group dance and teaching everyone a bit of popular Cuban culture made this an afternoon he would never forget.

By the time Mimi's mom had the delicious meal ready, we had all worked up a good appetite!

As we were sitting down, Mimi asked quietly if I would be willing to read my Cuban essay of thankfulness aloud to her family. I thought I would mispronounce words, or not be understood because of my accent, so I declined. Then she asked if she could read it to everyone after dinner. I told her I would feel honored, so she read it during dessert.

My story had certainly affected Agustín and me, but I was surprised to see that it also touched Mimi's family. Some of the women wiped away tears. I noticed that no one talked during the reading. They paid attention to every word as Mimi read, and several people asked me questions afterwards.

When the meal was over, the younger kids went outside to play kickball. Someone had brought a soccer ball, so Agustín and a few others formed two teams and began to play. Mimi led me to a small patio outside her room where we could be alone. I knew she had questions to ask, because we'd had no chance to speak in private since our essays had been turned in the day before.

"Rodolfo, I really like your story. It's heartbreaking, but it shows the life you and the others had to live under that horrible dictator, Fidel. What I want to know is, what was the straw that broke the camel's back? What made your parents know they had to send you here?"

I thought about it for a few moments; then I remembered the afternoon we saw a banker we knew.

"Mamá and I were walking home from the meat market, chatting as usual about our day. When we turned the corner to the park, we saw the body of a good friend of my parents—a banker—hanging limply from an oak tree. Mamá screamed and dropped her package. I grabbed her elbow and led her home. A police car cruised by, watching our reaction but doing nothing to remove the body."

Mimi's hand flew to her mouth, as if she might be sick. "Dear Lord," she whispered. "What did you do then?"

"My heart was pounding so loudly I couldn't think straight. I only knew I had to get my mother home. I guided her along the sidewalk to our house, and helped her lie down on the sofa. I told our nanny to call Papá right away."

The memory of that day still terrifies me; I will never forget the vivid image of that poor man, legs swaying gently in the breeze and hands hanging limply at his side.

Mimi moved closer to me. "Oh you poor thing. What happened to your mother?"

"Papá came home quickly and wrapped her in his arms. His eyes filled with tears when he saw the state she was in. Then we told him the story."

"Ay Dios Mío," he moaned, crossing himself emotionally. "My dear friend, Fernando, hanging from a park tree." He gulped for air as the tears spilled down his cheeks. "So now it's come to this," he groaned. "Enough is enough. The time has finally come."

Mimi reached over and squeezed my hand before rubbing it lightly.

"That's when he and Mamá began to organize our departure. Agustín and I didn't want to leave them, or our few friends still left in Cuba, but we knew their minds were made up."

With a long, weary sigh, Mimi looked intently at me.

"I'm so grateful your destiny led you here so we can help you four brave boys heal and enjoy life again. People here care for you. You know that, don't you?"

I couldn't think of anything to say. But I knew she was right. I put my arm around her and gathered her close to my heart. As she hugged me tightly, two of my tears dropped onto the front of her dress.

December 27, 1962

The final month of the year went by quickly. My English teacher entered my Cuba essay in a newspaper writing contest, and I won first prize: $25.00 from the *Staten Island Advance*. I took Mimi to the Statue of Liberty and invited Sergio, Agustín and Alberto to join us, but they said no so we could have a "special date." A few weeks later I visited it again with the guys. I am very interested in the history of the United States, and Ellis Island's story is motivating and energizing.

We kept calling our parents as often as possible, and let them know we had saved enough money from our jobs to fly them from Mexico to Miami. This became our shared project. No one was coming directly from Cuba to the United States, but we heard some Pedro Pan parents were getting through via Mexico.

Then we got some good news. Just before Christmas, and two months after the flights had stopped, Castro made a deal with the United States: he would release the one thousand one hundred-thirteen Bay of Pigs prisoners if the United States would pay a ransom of $53 million in food and medical supplies. This would be donated by companies from all over the U.S. But at the last minute, Fidel issued a new demand. He wanted $2.9 million in cash. Unbelievably, after Attorney General Robert F. Kennedy organized an intense fund-raising event, the prisoners were released.

On December 23, 1962, we four Cubans watched their arrival on television. Mrs. Jacqueline Kennedy met these men in Miami and addressed them in both English and Spanish in a heart-felt speech. We heard later that this act of kindness helped restore the Cuban people's faith in President Kennedy.

We also heard that some of the Pedro Pan parents had been able to board planes and ships returning after the delivery of supplies from the United States to Cuba. It happened so quickly; we had no chance to try and help our parents join that group.

I read in a newspaper article later that Americans living in Cuba, twenty-three American prisoners and over a thousand Cubans holding American citizenship were on the various return trips of these supply vessels.

After watching the release of the prisoners, we sat quietly, lost in our own thoughts. Agustín asked me why the Americans paid so much money to Fidel, when he was so evil. We tried to make sense of it, but never could.

Just before going to sleep that night, I made a decision. If those men who had been Castro's prisoners had made it back to the United States, then I was going to do whatever it took to bring my parents here. I felt more confident than I'd felt in a long time.

31

January 4, 1963

It's a new year and it's become very cold outside. We've never lived where it's this cold before, but we're learning to like it.

Fall with the changing colors of leaves was full of surprises. We examined them and discovered some were multi-colored. My favorites were the maple leaves, so I pressed a few in books to use as bookmarks. We all made piles of red and golden leaves to jump in and throw at each other. The cooler weather made playing outside lots of fun.

The first day it snowed, Agustín and I ran excitedly outdoors.

"Let's count them," I shouted. "Catch snowflakes on your tongue to see how they taste."

The next day enough snow fell for us to roll in. American kids who see this every year were ready to play with us, and showed us how to pack snowballs so they'd fly farther. By the end of the afternoon, we were expert snowball fighters—and needed to change into dry clothes.

And seeing my breath for the first time was incredible!

We're excited to spend the day with Mimi and her family tomorrow, and learn how to make taller snowmen. If there's enough snow we might even go sledding near her house!

I tell my parents they won't like the cold, but their reply is that they'll like anything as long as we're all together. Some of their friends have left Cuba to find flights to the U.S. from Mexico, Spain or Panama. Agustín and I urged them to do the same.

"Aunt Mercedes and Uncle Tomás are now in a small apartment in Mexico City. Your cousin Antonio left shortly after you two, so Uncle Tomás transferred ownership of all his factories to an army officer, in exchange for getting onto a flight to Mexico."

"Where is Antonio living now?"

"He's in Miami, in a foster home. He seems to like it okay."

"You should have been the ones to leave, Papá. You and Mamá already had your visas," complained Agustín. "It's not fair they left before you."

"Ay, *hijito* (little son). We don't have good contacts like my brother, nor the businesses to give someone. But your uncle will help us from Mexico. *No te preocupes* (don't worry)."

But we do worry. And pray. I sometimes feel guilty at the end of the day without having given a thought about my parents and their constant struggle. And we continue enjoying life more and more with our friends.

I told Agustín we need to think about them living with us soon in this new world, and helping them adjust once they arrive. It has been a real learning experience for all of us, which won't change once we are together again.

"When they finally get here, we will have to show them how life is in this country. That will be very difficult, especially for Papá, who always took good care of us."

"Will he be able to work here?" he asked me, coming up with something else to worry about.

"Probably not for a while, but one day he will. It will be a struggle for all of us, but they're our parents and have always done everything they could for us. Just think about all they've already given up, so you and I can be free."

Agustín added, "And they'll have to leave everything they've ever had: our house, our things, Papá's work and Mamá's jewelry, and even their country! All of this will stay behind in Cuba. Why don't we just go back and live with them there? I think . . ."

"Listen to me," I interrupted sternly. "You read my essay, and you know why. Life there gets worse every day. We could never live that way again, and they don't want us to. It's easier to give up material things than to surrender to a life that eats you up from the inside. That's why I worry about them."

Alberto and Sergio were devastated to learn that their father was imprisoned in Havana for being a *"rebelde"* (rebel). Their mother refused to leave him behind, so our buddies are afraid they may never see their parents again. We try to console them with words, but I cannot imagine their anxiety and fear. Sharing this pain has brought all of us closer, including Suzi and Mimi, who are very compassionate young women.

Mimi and I spend as much time together as possible, enjoying our last year of high school in each other's company almost daily. She's a star on her basketball team and has practice most afternoons. I go to as many games as possible, but I can't break curfew at *Mount Loretto*, so I have to miss night games during the week.

Saturdays we're always together, usually at her house. Sometimes Agustín joins us, but now he and Sergio have their own group of friends to hang out with in town. As long as they stay together, I don't worry about them.

Mimi and I talk about going to college. She's hoping to get a basketball scholarship from a New York college and has visited several of them with her parents. I have no idea what I'll do after graduation, or where we will live after my parents arrive. But I'm determined to find a school in New York State, which shouldn't be too expensive since we qualify as state residents. Most important is to be in the same city as Mimi, my brother, and my parents.

"Last weekend we visited the University of Rochester," Mimi tells me. "It's a small school with a great communications program, but I'm not sure it has a good athletic program. My dad wants me to go to Fordham, a Jesuit school in Manhattan with a very good athletic program. I like the idea of communications as a major, and their program is wonderful. What are you thinking about, Rodolfo?"

I shrugged. "I haven't even thought about it yet, with my parents' arrival still up in the air."

"But you need to apply in the spring if you want a scholarship. Why don't you look at the Staten Island Community College? It has a really good business administration program, and you told me you might like to study that. Why don't we check it out together?" she smiled, slipping her hand into mine.

"I like that idea. Next Saturday?"

"I'll pick you up at 11," she smiled. "Walk me to class?"

"Sure. Is it that time already?" Our lunch break always seems to fly by.

"Yes, it is. I'll see you after school, before my practice." She squeezed my hand and walked through the door to her next class.

32

March 6, 1963

James Baker found Monsignor Walsh engrossed in a spreadsheet showing the Catholic Welfare Bureau expenditures, his expression worried. When James cleared his throat, his friend looked up.

"Oh, hello there, James. How are you?" he asked, the familiar gracious smile a bit drawn.

"Just checking in, Bryan. How's life at Opa-locka?"

Bryan laughed. "It's never been harder, but now I realize how many more responsibilities a Monsignor has to deal with than a parish priest."

"I must say, your investiture ceremony at Miami Cathedral was the nicest one I've ever been to," James grinned. "Actually, it's the first one I've ever been to. It was quite an honor to be invited," he laughed, trying to lighten the mood.

Monsignor Walsh had known for some time that the shelters needed a new direction, and now he was in a position to define it. The details of such a change were taking up a lot of his time.

When flights between Cuba and the United States were cancelled in October 1962, the exodus of children from Cuba abruptly ended. The number of children in the camps was shrinking, since anyone who had turned nineteen had to leave the program and set out on their own. Monsignor Walsh decided to relocate foster-parent programs at Saint Raphael's and Florida City to meet the evolving needs of the still sizable population.

He rubbed his forehead, deep in thought. "You knew that in January I had to consolidate the shelters and move as many as I could to Opa-locka, since we can accommodate five hundred there."

"Yes, Bryan. Archbishop Coleman Carrol considered that the best solution. There are better facilities, several dining rooms, recreational areas, twelve classrooms and even a chapel, but it's much harder to administrate than your smaller camps."

"You can say that again! But fortunately, the good Lord has sent us six Marist brothers and thirty-four lay people to teach them."

"How do your Saint Raphael boys feel about the move?"

"Well, at first they were furious. They didn't like the barracks, the open showers, and the lack of privacy. But since I'm now there with them, they've accepted it and I believe some even like it."

"What happened to the girls?"

"They've all been moved to Florida City. There are fewer of them, and no one else is arriving. Everything will work out as it's meant to. As reluctant as I've been to share numbers and other identifying information on the children, it doesn't seem to matter now."

"Remember when the press wrote that Castro would rather have Havana get the dollars for the airplane tickets than have the kids there?"

"I do. That was when the press decided that *Operation Pedro Pan* was a secret plot to prevent Fidel Castro from halting the exodus. Our press conferences laying out the humanitarian aspects of the program supported the U.S. government's policies."

"Bryan, I'm still ambivalent about how the press has interpreted our good intentions. They sometimes seem to be conspiring with the government to misinform the public."

"Which is why we must continue to be as transparent as possible, now that the children are here. When the newspapers unfairly complain that we refuse to discuss the Cuban side of the story, we can truthfully say we have no communication with the Cuban government or incentive to express their point of view."

"Monsignor, you are the most open-minded person I know. As long as this program is in your hands, it will be run fairly and efficiently." He paused.

"Which reminds me of something I've heard several times. Some boys are referring to you as the 'second St. Patrick.' Do you remember how that got started?"

Bryan nodded with a wide grin. "Indeed I do. There was a young man in Matecumbe who was chosen to go to Saint Rafael but refused, telling us he wouldn't go without his younger brother. I met with him and told him if he were well behaved for the next two weeks there, he could bring his brother to Saint Rafael as soon as there was an opening."

"And did he go?"

"Yes, and in two weeks exactly, there was an opening and his younger brother joined him. Now they are both here in Opa-locka, the newest camp, and they've started referring to me as 'the second St. Patrick.'"

"Someday when I write your biography," James Baker said expansively, "I will also include the 'fire alarm' story."

"Who told you that one? Did I?"

"You told me some boys had pulled the alarm at Saint

Rafael on All Innocents Day at 6:00 a.m. But you failed to mention that the firemen came and it cost the shelter $200. So the following Friday, when you handed out allowances, the boys noticed coins in the envelope. That was a surprise, since you usually gave them two one-dollar bills. They thought they were getting a raise, but inside the envelopes each boy found only $1.75."

Monsignor Walsh laughed loudly. "The looks on their faces was priceless. When they asked me why I told them, 'the fire department's fine for the false alarm was $200, so I deducted from all of your allowances.'"

"That's one thing we admire and like about you. The punishment always fits the crime, and you are a fair and reasonable leader."

"James, would you like to get some lunch with me? I know a very good and cheap place."

They walked out of the office and into the beautiful spring day. The March sunshine gave the morning a glow as golden as a ripe peach. A sudden sweet aroma of wisteria washed over them—the very scent of Cuba.

"Bryan, this is how Havana smelled. I feel as if I'm back there," James reminisced. "Look at the fuchsia and white azaleas, and those beautiful daffodils, dancing with the tulips. I feel like I stepped back in time, which makes me a little anxious."

"You've been working too hard. And you probably haven't eaten all day. We're almost there." He took his friend's arm to cross the street toward a diner. "Tell me, do you still have friends in Cuba?'

James shook his head. "Everyone I knew in the clergy and in the schools has left. Some of my students might remain, but I've lost contact with them. I barely think about those days, but today it just came rushing back."

They sat down at the table and ordered their lunch. James' mood improved, and he asked about the Socarras brothers.

"Have you heard from them lately?" he wondered.

Bryan Walsh's face lit up. "Just yesterday," he answered. "How did you know? And they asked me to give you their best wishes, so perhaps you are a bit intuitive."

James smiled. "What did they write about their lives?"

"Their parents haven't arrived yet, but are trying to come in through Mexico. Rodolfo has a girlfriend, as does Alberto Ochoa. They are both looking into going to state colleges next year, and asked if I would be a reference for them. Of course I agreed."

Then he spoke more softly. "Poor Alberto's father is imprisoned in Havana, so they asked me for prayers for his release." He pensively remembered what Rodolfo had written: '*The light at the end of the tunnel often seems so far away.*'

"They must need lots of encouragement, with their lives still unsettled."

"Yes, that's why I wrote: '*Never surrender hope that you will live with your parents again one day.*'"

James nodded in agreement. "I do miss those four, and many of the other Pedro Pans. It's like an enormous family spinning off in many directions. Sometimes I feel weary of so much change. I pray for more stability."

Monsignor Walsh smiled. "My friend, what we all want is a simple revelation in which all is known, all is forgiven, and everything left can be celebrated with a victory cheer. That is why we work so hard and so well together in our program."

"Bryan, I just realized what brought me to your office this morning. Last night I dreamed about the day we first met. It was December of 1960, and I told you about my idea of establishing a boarding school for the children we would bring out of Cuba. Do you remember what you told me?"

"Not really, except that I discouraged you from starting the school."

"You explained that the Catholic Welfare Bureau would get federal funds for housing the children and that only licensed child-placing agencies would be involved. But most compelling was your comparison of the benefits of foster care over institutional care, based on the importance to the Cuban parents of safeguarding their children's religious heritage."

"Which we've been able to do, haven't we, James?"

"Thanks to your foresight and awareness, along with your sincere desire to find a solution. That's what convinced me that day that your idea was much better than mine." Grinning, he added, "And I re-lived that entire meeting in my dream last night."

"Our admiration is mutual, my friend. I don't believe we would have been able to do this without each other."

James Baker nodded. "I concur, Bryan." His eyes glanced over his shoulder. "Here comes our food. I will pray for us, for the boys, and for His bounty and love."

"Thank you, James."

33

March 10, 1963

Today is my birthday, and I feel totally celebrated. Yesterday Mimi threw me a surprise birthday party at her home. She'd somehow even arranged for the four of us to return to *Mount Loretto* after curfew (her father drove us back to the orphanage shortly before 10 p.m.)

Alberto had given Mimi a list of my closest friends, and she asked Sergio and Agustín to invite one friend each. She had her own list of friends and family. A total of twenty-eight people came, along with a few adults. Her parents cooked us a delicious pot roast for dinner.

Afterwards some of us danced to the newest Beatles' album, "Please, Please Me" while others played card games or dominos in small groups. A few even brought gifts, which I opened later. It was really fun—Mimi pulled off a great party. She's the best!

"How did you guys keep this secret from me?" I asked the others in the car, surprised that they managed it.

"Mimi blackmailed us," grinned Agustín. "She said if you found out, we wouldn't get to go ice skating with them next weekend." Ice skating was one of the new sports we'd taken up. We rented skates inexpensively right near the rink.

Mamá and Papá phoned us this morning during breakfast, and Agustín and I spoke with them for about ten minutes. They finally have their airline tickets to Mexico! They also received the money we had saved up from our jobs and allowances. They'll fly to Mexico City at the end of the month and stay at the same apartment where my aunt and uncle lived for about forty days. There are other Cuban couples living in that building, and they know one family there. I am so thankful that they are getting out of Cuba, but also concerned about how they will be able to pay for rent and food.

"*No se preocupen, queridos* (don't worry, my dears)," Mamá replied to our many questions. "*Dios* (God) will show us the way."

Monsignor Walsh sent us the names and phone numbers of two Cuban families who live on Staten Island and wanted to meet us, so we invited them over. Monsignor Walsh had met them a few months ago and believes they will help us and our parents when they arrive.

I cannot imagine how that good man always finds solutions to every problem. The last time we spoke, he told us there were now over fourteen thousand Pedro Pans living in the United States, and I'm pretty sure he's helped every single one of us.

Monsignor Walsh also told me that because I'm now nineteen, I will only be able to stay here until school ends in June. Then we have to make a decision about our futures. Agustín and Sergio can stay here for another three years, but Alberto and I will graduate and are applying to college, so we'll probably begin living on or near a college campus. Hopefully we'll be accepted at the same college and can room together.

Not knowing when our parents will get here, we've

talked with James Baker, Monsignor Walsh and the priests at *Mount Loretto* about the best course of action. Ideally the younger brothers can continue living here, while Alberto and I apply for scholarships to New York colleges that would cover our tuition and living expenses. Everyone thinks that will be easy thanks to our good grades. We'll also need to get part-time jobs, which shouldn't be too difficult.

Right now, our spiritual leaders tell us to "give it to God" and we are. We've both applied to two colleges in New York City, hoping to get accepted (with scholarships) to at least one together.

Mimi and I continue sharing our lives and time. She's like an angel to me. Her understanding, compassion, and love of life have really lifted me up when I've been down. This is my first romantic relationship, and I'm still learning how to share what's inside me with her. She knows all about my interrupted Cuban childhood and appreciates how that life still calls to me. My dream is to never let her go—to spend our lives together. Such dreams keep me inspired and energized, and I definitely treasure this one. I pray we can make it work.

My brother, Alberto and Sergio enjoyed meeting the Cuban couples. They arrived after lunch recently and joined us in the living area. They are from Havana, and arrived here with their children about five years earlier, even before Fidel took over the country. They escaped early, fleeing Batista's cruel regime.

"My wife, Ana, and I brought our two small children here, because we feared that our lives would become more difficult in Cuba," explained Mario Martínez. "I was a physician in Havana and knew I could eventually get my medical degree accepted here, which I have. It was a difficult decision, but at least we could leave quietly and establish our new lives in New York."

Ana also shared some experiences and feelings.

"Our children are ten and eight, growing up as American children. Sometimes we regret that they're losing so much of our Cuban background and heritage, but we know this was the right decision to make. When life crumbles around you, you have to take survival actions."

María Teresa Santiago came a year later, with her husband Roberto. They knew some of the same people in Havana—friends of our parents.

"We also knew Ana and Mario in Havana; my husband was in accounting and business. He managed the main office of Banco Nacionál in Havana. We communicated with Mario and Ana and they convinced us to leave everything and come with them. We read the writing on the wall about what was happening in Cuba, and decided to leave our homeland."

"Has it been very difficult?" asked Alberto.

"In the beginning. Now we've assimilated, but we'll always have a place in our hearts for Cuba, her people and her customs. We don't know if we can ever go back to live, or even visit, but that is our hope. We have family there we want to see. Now they cannot join us nor can we return . . . perhaps one day."

Her husband added, "Sometimes it feels like being in suspended animation. I'm sad some days to think I don't belong to Cuba anymore. I wanted to live there forever, but circumstances changed that. Some days I don't feel Cuban, or American either." He shrugged, "It's a wound we'll always carry."

I asked if they had children. "We adopted a teenage girl here two years ago, and now she's learning Spanish," he grinned. "She's given us a reason to be happy and grateful. We'd love for you to meet her one day."

When they left, we agreed this was not a coincidence, but one more gift sent our way. We believed they would keep a watch over us. As they hugged us goodbye, they also volunteered to help our parents make the adjustments when they finally got here.

34

June 30, 1963

So much has happened this month: high school graduation, college acceptances, scholarship offers, and a summer job. The only thing we haven't celebrated is our parents' arrival, because that hasn't happened yet.

We were really hoping our parents would be here in time for our high school graduation, but none of them could make it. The good news is that Alberto and Sergio's father has been released from prison! Now his parents are desperately trying to get out of Cuba. Mamá and Papá are still in Mexico City, waiting for their U.S. visas.

When we last heard from them, they seemed calmer and almost upbeat. "We're looking into this, and with new friends and local churches helping us out financially, we are not suffering at all. We'll be there to embrace you soon, *amados hijos* (beloved sons). Pray for us!" Mamá's voice was choked with emotion.

To show we believe they will be here soon, Alberto and I have put our large graduation photos in an album to give our parents.

Agustín was still miserable when we went to bed that evening. "Rodolfo, we haven't seen Mamá and Papá for more than a year, and I don't think they'll ever be able to come," he sniffed.

I wrapped my arms around him. "Don't say that, *hermanito*. Some friends haven't seen their parents since 1960, and still believe they will come. Please don't lose your faith. I need you to believe they will get here, and remind me when I have doubts of my own."

He wiped away a tear and hugged me back. "I will, Rodolfo, but my heart hurts and I feel like I can't really get on with my life until we have our parents here."

"I understand that. But we have to work together to stay strong when they arrive. Remember, they'll depend on us in this country. On both of us."

Agustín quickly agreed. He probably just wanted to feel needed.

Mimi's family threw a high school graduation party and invited many of our friends with some of their family members. The big surprise was the limo she rented to take us all to her house! It waited while we were eating dinner, then drove us around New York City to see the sights.

We didn't return until midnight! Luckily, Mimi's family had gotten the orphanage curfew changed for us again. I don't know how they did it, but Mimi usually gets what she wants. Our brothers came along for the limo ride, very excited to share that unique experience.

Mimi was the first one of us to be accepted to the school of her choice: Fordham University at the Rose Hill campus. She's in the Liberal Arts program, with a major in communications, and hopes to play basketball on the college team.

Alberto and I were both accepted at Staten Island Community College, and we each received scholarships from the Liberal Arts and Science programs. The *Staten Island Advance* ran an article about local students who had received scholarships; our profile was captioned "*Cuban Boys Win Scholarships for Their Excellent Scholastic*

Achievements." I know our parents will be very proud to see this, so Alberto and I put copies of the article in large envelopes along with the other graduation mementos.

Alberto dreams of being the first Cuban astronaut—after getting his undergraduate degree, of course. I'm not sure what I want to study, but science will probably be necessary for either law, history or medicine so I'll begin with that. It's inspiring to know we're going to the same college and can share living quarters.

And the best part of it is that Mimi will be only forty minutes away, and has a car! It was her graduation present from her parents—a generous gift I'll also benefit from. I am a lucky guy.

Alberto asked one question I couldn't answer. "If your parents get here before we go to school, will you find a place for them, with you and Agustín?"

"*Amiguito*, (little friend), I hadn't even thought about that. If your folks aren't here by then, why not get an apartment for all of us?"

He laughed. "Another question for Padre Palá or Father Kehan, I guess. But thanks for including me in your future housing plans."

Alberto and I landed summer jobs at a small medical center, walking distance from the orphanage. There are two working shifts, so sometimes we have the day shift together and other weeks one of us will work afternoons and the other from 6:00 a.m. to 2:00 p.m. We're getting paid well for this work, and even though we've just started, we're learning a lot about surgery, medications and health care.

"Alberto, I'm happy they're letting us stay at *Mount Loretto* until August. I'm pretty sure Monsignor Walsh had something to do with that, aren't you?"

He nodded enthusiastically. "I'm sure he did. But

remember, I'm still eligible to live here, since I'm only eighteen!" He smiled happily. "Rodolfo, we are so blessed. Just think, less than two years ago we had no idea of what we would find here, and were missing our families like crazy. And now . . . life's almost perfect."

He suddenly turned serious, thinking about our absent parents. Soon . . . please God, soon.

"Hey, you'll be close to Suzi too. Isn't she going to nursing school in Brooklyn? You can get together every weekend." I still couldn't believe we'd actually have our girlfriends close enough to visit so often. Something else to be thankful for.

Our brothers will attend the same high school and graduate in two years. Certainly our parents will be with us by then! In the meantime, no need to worry about Agustín and Sergio. We're hoping they will find part-time jobs they enjoy.

Since our tuition is completely covered, Alberto and I will start looking for a cheap apartment near campus. We can buy food and learn to cook, or work in the college cafeteria for discounted meals. We know we'll need part-time jobs, and that sounds like a good one. With the money we'll save this summer, we're feeling confident about becoming independent.

September 25, 1963

By September, Alberto and I were very worried about our parents coming to the U.S. We called Monsignor Walsh to see if he could help us feel better.

"My sons, you know that *Operation Pedro Pan* officially

ended last October. Our good friend, Wendell Rollason, was still able to get fraudulent documents, including visas, to get the underground fighters out of Cuba. But unfortunately he's been arrested in Mexico, so he can no longer help us."

"What about my parents, Monsignor? Are they still on his list to get out?" asked Alberto, afraid of what the answer might be.

"We can't say for sure, Alberto. Rollason was our contact and still has influential friends in all three countries, including the Episcopalian bishop here in Miami. He told me the bishop is organizing a campaign to get him out of jail."

"And what's happening in Mexico, Monsignor? Why has everything stopped?" I asked.

"Rodolfo, you know the State Department and the Immigration Service are the ones to issue those visas, and they move in mysterious ways. But try not to worry. The parents and family members won't be forgotten. Several lawyers in Mexico are helping us organize transit visas for Cubans with unaccompanied children in the United States. Soon there will be more of them. All we can do is wait . . . and pray."

Monsignor Walsh cleared his throat, "Boys, there are no guarantees that refugees can work when they arrive to the United States. I do know personally of many cases where doctors are working as janitors and lawyers are packing boxes in factories. But, some professionals have been able to return to their careers after passing exams in the field."

"Even if they don't speak English?" asked Alberto.

"The language barrier has been difficult for some, yet many have persevered to master English and pass the qualifying examinations."

We thanked him and tried to concentrate on our studies. We had saved enough money over the summer to open a bank account for our parents and help them get settled. But some days were much tougher than others.

Agustín and I got an optimistic phone call from Mamá and Papá on a Saturday afternoon, while Mimi was visiting us at *Mount Loretto*. They told us they had just moved from the crowded apartment to a small room in a hotel. For $120.00 a month, they also got breakfast and lunch. Mamá offered to cook and teach the staff some new Cuban recipes for a little money. And a Christian Mexican lawyer agreed to work on their visa case *pro bono.*

"Por fin, hijos, ya tenemos fé que Dios nos dará la manera para salir. (Finally boys, we have faith that God will show us the way out)."

We were happy and ready to believe them, yet kept praying and asking our priest friends to do the same.

"Rodolfo, my family is also praying for the four of you, and I've asked my girlfriends to do the same. I really believe it is going to happen soon. Don't you?" Mimi assured me when I hung up the phone.

I gathered her into my arms and kissed her with passion. Her lips were warm. She was so surprised she kissed me back.

"Yes, Mimi. It's strange, but that phone call gave me real hope. And with so many prayers, I know God will answer them."

I slipped my arms around her and nuzzled her neck. She let out a laugh that was tinged with wonder. We were finally close to peace.

35

October 26, 1963

Mimi and her parents had never been to Cuba, but today they got a sense of how joyfully relatives and neighbors in Havana celebrate the arrival of beloved family members, especially after a long separation.

Two days earlier my parents had flown from Mexico City to Miami and stayed with relatives so they could catch their breath and be ready for our unforgettable reunion. We bought them tickets to New York City so they would arrive on a weekend, and we could all pick them up. Mimi drove Agustín, Alberto, Sergio and me; her parents followed us so there would be room for everyone.

Since arriving in the United States, we had only spoken with our parents through letters and phone calls. Agustín and I had managed to get through a year and a half without them, but it was difficult. Now we will be able to introduce them to the American way of life. My parents will expect us to live with them until we marry as we would have at home.

Alberto and I have rented an apartment near campus and our younger brothers are comfortable in *Mount Loretto*, but we will look for a place not far from Agustin's school and my college so we can all be together. Mimi's uncle owns a small rental house and has given us a very fair price for at least a month. I'll stay there with them until they feel settled and we have a more permanent solution.

Life will be very different now that we are older and accustomed to living here, but at least we can hug them before leaving for school, and share *abrazos* again when we return. We can kiss them goodnight. Every night. We can dance the Salsa and go shopping together, reminiscing about happy times and friends and life before Castro.

Yes, it will be different, but Cubans have always found ways to make the best of what we have. The nervous yet optimistic feeling of anticipation that was tying my stomach in knots was something I've felt before—the day I last saw my parents.

"They've landed, *hermano*," Agustín shouted. People are walking this way. Can you see them?"

My hand suddenly turned sweaty holding Mimi's, and I realized I was trembling. I closed my eyes for a moment and breathed deeply.

"*Mamá, Papá, estamos aquí!* (We're over here!)" Agustín was running toward them and flying into Papá's arms. I rushed to Mamá and held her in a long embrace.

"Rodolfo, my beloved son. Please promise me we'll never be separated again," were her first words. Her emotional hug almost stopped my breath as she kept repeating through sobs, "Please, please promise me." She was praying for an end to all the pain.

As Papá wrapped me in a big hug, I buried my face in his shirt, where our tears mixed. I could feel his rapid heartbeat. My wonderful caring father had never been this emotional in public, and I felt deeply moved.

Mimi and her parents were moved also as they waited to be introduced. Wiping away tears, they all hugged and murmured greetings and welcomes. Our parents felt the genuinely mixed emotions of Alberto and Sergio, and gave them strong hugs on behalf of their absent parents.

Papá looked thinner; his hair had turned grey, his shoulders slumped forward, and his face carried many wrinkles, although he was only forty-seven. His familiar brown suit drooped from his shoulders. He looked tired and weary after the long trip and much longer separation.

Mamá hadn't changed much, but the brightly flowered dress I had always loved seemed too large now. Her eyes were not as animated as I remembered, probably because of all the tears. Her skin was paler than before, but she hadn't lost her beauty. Her hair—always perfectly coiffed—now fell loosely around her face. I gave her another hug and told her she looked beautiful.

"Ay Rodolfo, we've changed quite a bit. But so have you two! Look at how tall Agustín is now! And you, my son, are such a handsome young man."

An affectionate smile warmed her expression as she turned again to Mimi and her parents. "Thank you so much for caring about my boys. They've told me about your warm support, and how you make them feel at home. I don't think we can ever repay you." That was the longest English expression I'd ever heard from her, so I was sure she'd been practicing it. Relieved and content, I hugged her again.

Mamá had been right, I thought, as we walked to get their suitcases. I too was a different person—more independent, resourceful and better at solving problems. All of the Pedro Pans were. We turned problems into possibilities and possibilities into hopes in our determined search of brighter futures. My parents' physical presence is an important part of my new reality. Now that we're all reunited, it is the sons' turn to support the parents.

Mimi and her family plus Alberto and Sergio dropped us off at the rental house. Mimi promised to come back later to pick us up for dinner at her house.

In the furnished living room, we sat together on the sofa to look through the scrapbook I had put together: my graduation certificate and scholarship papers, Mothers' and Fathers' Day cards, newspaper clippings, a beautiful picture Agustín had drawn, photographs of us and a copy of my essay.

"This is our welcome gift for you, to show how we've kept you with us all this time. You can look at it more carefully later, but it's something Agustín and I made for you both."

Mamá's eyes shone brightly. "*Es el major regalo, hijos míos.* (It's the best gift ever, my sons). We will treasure this forever."

We are together at last. What seemed like a dream so long ago has finally come true. We have all survived and are stronger because of it. And we are a united family once again.

Gracias a Dios.

EPILOGUE

Alberto and Sergio Ochoa's parents finally arrived to New York City on a *Freedom Flight* in February of 1966. Alberto graduated college and was enrolled in medical school at Columbia University with a full scholarship. After high school, he had never lost touch with Suzi, and they married while he was still in medical school.

Sergio lived with his parents in an apartment in New York City while studying at Brooklyn College. His degree was in journalism, and he became a reporter for *The New York Times*. Their parents taught together in a New York City bilingual school. They never returned to Cuba.

Rodolfo Socarras studied immigration law as an undergraduate, with a full scholarship to prestigious New York University. Four years later he got a degree from NYU's School of Law. He and Mimi married and moved to Greenwich Village, where Rodolfo practiced immigration law. Mimi put her communication's degree to good use as a writer for *Glamour Magazine*. They eventually raised three children in upstate New York.

Agustín Socarras lived with his parents in the same house they originally rented from Mimi's uncle. His father, after a year of study, became a licensed contractor. His mother loved the city's buildings and homes, studied to be a realtor and eventually received her broker's license.

Agustín's analytical mind led him to a degree in engineering at Yale School of Engineering and Applied Science, also with a full scholarship. Their parents were extremely proud of Rodolfo and Agustín, their wonderful wives, and their five grandchildren. They always prayed for the end of the Castro regime, so they could take their grandchildren to Cuba and show them their heritage.

The Escobár family stayed in Beaverton, Oregon to finish out the school year. During this time, Señor Escobár worked in construction and studied to re-instate his pharmaceutical degree in the U.S. Señora Escobár worked in the kitchen in a nearby grammar school.

In August of 1962, they left Oregon and rented a house in Miami, sharing it with their grandparents, who had arrived from Cuba three months earlier. Within the year, Señor Escobár worked again as a licensed pharmacist. Liliana and Diego enjoyed high school in Miami, and both attended the Florida State University College of Law in Tallahassee, Florida.

Liliana met Miguel Rocha in law school and married him after graduation. They remained in Tallahassee, where they raised their three daughters. Her husband, Miguel, served as vice-president on the Board of the Catholic Charities of the Orlando Diocese and traveled often, while Liliana worked as an immigration attorney in Tallahassee. In 2000, she ran and won the seat of Florida Senator: an honor she and Mel Martínez shared. He was the first Pedro Pan United States Senator from Florida; she the first Pedro Pan Florida Senator. They enjoyed sharing their memories when they attended the same events. *

Diego worked in human rights law in Tallahassee, and lived close to his sister and parents. He never married, but thoroughly enjoyed spoiling his nieces. He was chosen by Florida Governor Charlie Crist to be his Chief of Staff, and later returned to his law practice.

Today nearly 2.2 million Cubans (out of a total population

of 11.3 million) live in the United States. There is something of a divide between the Cubans who left and those who stayed. Some believe those who stayed contributed to Cuba becoming what it is now, by inadvertently bolstering and legitimizing Castro's power through their silence.

Havana is a beautiful city shrouded in sadness, belied by a jubilant air of optimism. Its atmosphere often gives the impression that life is a tremendous holiday. But most Cubans feel like guests in their own country, in a society "on loan" from Fidel.

Although not satisfied with their standard of living, they realize their lives are slowly changing. Meaningful opportunities remain elusive, yet the economy is gradually improving. Harsh reality and the relentless struggle continue.

How many people on both sides have looked across the water and yearned for something they can't have—a family member, their country, a lost love, the soil where they walked, the air they breathed?

A Cuban gentleman was asked what his dream for Cuba is. "Free. Democratic. I would like to be able to protest when I do not agree with what my government is doing, without fear of reprisal. To own something the government can't take from me, and to be my own person. This government keeps us so preoccupied with the daily struggle that there's very little time and energy left to take control of our future. Fidel has shown us the cost of our silence."

Most Cuban exiles living in America say they will not return until the country becomes a democracy.

*While the protagonists in the story are based on the true lives of some of the Petro Pan children, the characters themselves are fictitious and any resemblance they bear to actual people is a coincidence.

AFTERWORD

The early 1960s were the best of times and the worst of times for Cubans.

In the fall of 1963, the State Department estimated that between nine and ten thousand people in Cuba holding visa waivers had unaccompanied children or spouses living in the United States. Volunteer agencies caring for the children asked the *American Council of Volunteer Agencies for Foreign Service* to draw up a list of priority cases.

They then petitioned the State Department for permission to allow these persons to relocate to the United States. The State Department's answer was: *While sympathetic, the proposal is not feasible because of higher security needs (blockade) and also because of the difficulty in setting priorities and securing the co-operation of Cuba.*

On November 22, 1963, President John F. Kennedy was assassinated, and Vice President Lyndon Johnson assumed the presidency. JFK's policy had relied on the *Monroe Doctrine* to justify its sanctions against Cuba, and Johnson—who had chaired meetings of the National Security Council that oversaw Cuba policy—followed the same approach.

In Miami, there was local pressure to get the exiles resettled in other parts of the country. 50,000 refugees had been relocated, but an estimated 125,000 remained in Miami. Given these numbers, President Johnson was adamant that renewed immigration from Cuba was not to be encouraged.

But the pressure to leave Cuba increased when Castro

called for compulsory military duty for all boys. No one under fifteen would be given exit permits because induction to the military began at age seventeen. Even though *Operation Pedro Pan* had ended, Monsignor Walsh continued to help the Catholic Church in Cuba get the children out via Spain or other countries.

By late September of 1965, Fidel Castro agreed to allow Cubans already in the United States to pick up relatives on the island. He opened up the port of Camarioca, a small fishing port west of Havana, on October 10. President Johnson announced that people seeking refuge in the United States would be welcomed. He signed a reform of the U.S. Immigration Law, in which he stated that he would ask Congress for $13.6 million to pay for it.

Approximately one thousand boats originating from Miami made the trip to Camarioca. Those leaving Cuba were forced to abandon their homes and turn other assets and belongings over to the government. 2,979 Cubans left from Camarioca, and the 2,104 Cubans remaining when Camarioca was closed on October 28 were transported to Florida on boats chartered by the United States, at a tremendous cost.

The next few months were filled with tension for the Pedro Pan children and their families. Negotiations continued to achieve an orderly exodus. In early November, Fidel Castro made a surprising announcement: he would allow Cubans to travel to the U.S. and Cubans living there to return to visit the island. An intense diplomatic war raged for several months. The Swiss embassy became the intercessor, relaying messages back and forth. The Americans proposed that first priority be given to the 15,000 to 20,000 Cubans with relatives in the U.S. and second priority to the 15,000 to 30,000 political prisoners.

The greatest disagreement was about exactly who could leave Cuba. Political prisoners languishing in Cuban jails could be exchanged for a pledge of noninterference by the United States. Finally, it was agreed that priority would be given to Cubans with relatives in the U.S., stressing the importance of reuniting divided families. And Cuba insisted that young men aged fifteen to twenty-six would not leave.

On November 5th, both governments signed a *Memorandum of Understanding*. The unaccompanied children's plight would be the justification for opening the doors for a new wave of Cuban exiles. Camarioca had been closed so the United States would be allowed to set up two flights a day, the so-called *Freedom Flights*.

Every day beginning December 1, 1965, two planes filled with refugees departed Veradero, Cuba for the United States. The highest priority was given to parents with minor children in the United States. Seven airlines operated the *Freedom Flights*. The U.S. government provided a $100 resettlement grant for each family or $60 per individual, in addition to paying for the flights to and from Cuba.

During December of 1965, the parents of 128 children arrived on the *Freedom Flights*. The following month, that number increased to 456. These twice-daily, five-days-a-week *Freedom Flights* lasted until February 1, 1973. They cost the federal government $50 million dollars.

Fortunately for many Pedro Pans, this was the end of their lengthy separations from their parents. Yet sadly, not all divided families were reunited. The Pedro Pans who were nineteen and had left the program could not be accounted for, and some of their statistics aren't available.

For the Pedro Pans with parents still in Cuba, there was no possibility of visits. The proposal allowing Cubans access between both countries was dropped. While the United States allowed refugees in, it prohibited travel back to Cuba. Castro refused to allow re-entry for those who had left. Now the only hope for the unaccompanied children was their parents' arrival in the U.S. In 1973, Castro ordered the doors shut again. Because young men of military age could not leave the country, families had to decide between leaving Cuba or staying behind with their sons.

In the twenty months between December 26, 1960 and October 23, 1962, over 14,000 unaccompanied minors arrived in Miami under the sponsorship of the Catholic Welfare Bureau. These children were from all over the island, mostly from middle-and lower-class families, and from various racial backgrounds, including Black and Chinese. While the majority was Catholic, several hundred were Protestant, Jewish or non-believers.

Almost ninety percent of the children who were in the custody of the Catholic Welfare Bureau were reunited with their parents by June, 1966. No children were placed for adoption, since the purpose of the program was to safeguard parental rights. Every effort was made to avoid publicity and propaganda. *Operation Pedro Pan* was formed to protect the Cuban children from the Marxist-Leninist indoctrination, after the experience of the literacy program of 1960 and the closure of Catholic and private schools. The Catholic Welfare Bureau provided a means for Cuban parents to exercise their fundamental human right to direct their children's education.

ACKNOWLEDGMENTS

No man is an island. No writer writes alone. Completing a book is never easy. When you find some aspect of writing that presents a new challenge, it can be frustrating, exhausting and terrifying. But in the end, it's exhilarating. Sometimes the greatest pleasure in writing comes from finding a way through those challenges.

This novel has been a labor of love to write, and it holds a special place in my heart.

I would like to acknowledge and express my deep gratitude to my superb book team. To my editor, Carey "Trip" Giudici, I offer heartfelt thanks for steering me past the pitfalls and keeping my feet grounded. Thank you for your wonderful sense of humor while dealing with my harried author's nerves. Your critical counsel over the fourteen years we've worked together has made all the difference in my novels. Thank you for bringing renewed energy to my writing.

Kudos to my esteemed artists: Gini Steele and Patty Osborne. I give Gini my concept about the cover art, she grasps it and provides it! I do believe you "can judge a book by the cover," and I'm very picky about what I like. Thank you so much for giving me just what I wanted! Then my patient and accomplished "bookmaker" Patty Osborne takes Gini's art work and wields her magic wand, making the books even more beautiful than I expected. You awesome ladies have never let me down. Please accept my heartfelt thanks.

I am also very grateful to my additional readers—four incredibly talented proof readers who read and weeded out the typos and errors, and tightened up my writing. Thank you for offering your criticism in a way that felt almost complimentary. These special ladies are Cathy Drury, Suzi Hassel, Diane Knight, and Cassandra Coveney, my daughter. Cassandra's experience with leaving a country she loved to move to an unknown land paralleled Liliana's story in many ways, and her understanding of a thirteen-year-old child's mind brought a tender perspective to the story. Thank you all for doing an outstanding job, including working overtime to meet our deadline.

Hats off to my research partners, Suzi Hassel and Ruthie Miller. I owe you two so much and thank you for the fun we had driving all over Miami to do critical research for this complex book. Sometimes we even split up and worked in different places to get the job done. We visited universities, libraries, historical foundations, museums and some terrific restaurants, laughing and learning all the way. Thank you, Ruthie and Bill Miller, for being the perfect hosts and opening up your home in Ft. Lauderdale to Suzi and me.

A very special thank you to the women who granted me interviews, told me their own stories and generously offered research material assistance. Several Pedro Pans requested to remain anonymous, yet shared their time and inspiring stories with me, through emails and personal interviews. I could never have written this novel without their valuable assistance.

Maria Dominguez got me started on this journey, for which I am so grateful. Thank you for telling me your story and introducing me to the Pedro Pan stories.

I am indebted and so grateful to Ximena Valdivia, the manager of the *Barry University Archives and Special*

Collections. Ximena opened the library to me and shared an invaluable collection—the *Monsignor Bryan O. Walsh Papers.* They document the private and public life of Monsignor Walsh between 1948 through 2001. Ximena and I are frequently in e-mail communication, and she answers my requests graciously and promptly. Thank you so much for your helpful contributions and your support.

I want to offer deep respect and admiration to all the Pedro Pan families, who entrusted their children's fate to governmental and religious organizations in the United States. Their leap of faith gave their children hope, freedom and new opportunities. Thank you for your courage.

As always, I want to thank my family for their patience and encouragement. To my daughters Cassandra and Ticiana, thank you for being such caring daughters. Pieces of you and your children usually somehow end up in the characters of my books. To my amazing mother, Phyllis Bauer, thank you for your loving support and belief in me and my work. Thank you for praying over your five children. And thank you for gracing this world for 99 years, and still remaining the loving and beautiful woman you are.

Last on the list, but first in my heart, is my beloved husband Michael, who is always there with his boundless emotional support and encouragement. Dear Mike, thank you for making me laugh every day. Your confidence in me is treasured. You never questioned my passion for this story, and you walked by my side and held my hand as I wrote it.

I offer my deepest thanks to God, who has given me the words to share, and has woven my life and art into a beautiful tapestry. Thank You for the comfort of Your Spirit, and Your grace to all mankind. May this story honor You.

BOOK GROUP DISCUSSION QUESTIONS

1. When Liliana and Diego's parents left them in the airport behind the glass enclosure, what was your emotional reaction? Could you understand their motivations? Did your understanding grow as the novel progressed?

2. How important a role do you believe that their faith played throughout the novel? What do you think was most essential to the children in their survival?

3. Had you ever heard about the Pedro Pans before reading this story? Did learning their story surprise you? In what way?

4. Who is your favorite character in the novel? Did you identify as easily with the children as with Father Walsh or James Baker? What might you have done differently if you were them?

5. What did you think of the shelter system used by the Catholic Welfare Bureau to house the children? Do you believe all options were considered?

6. The children wanted to shield their parents from the truth of camp life. Do you feel that was the most caring thing for them to do? Why or why not?

7. Discuss the relationship Father Walsh had with the children. Did he meet their needs? Do you believe he might have dealt with them differently?

8. Which version of choosing the name *Pedro Pan* for their program do you prefer? The Peter Pan story, or the fifteen year-old boy Pedro who asked Father Walsh for bread (*pan*)? Why?

9. Do you think the children's memories were accurate and reliable? What does this suggest about how time influences our perspective? How does the past affect our future?

10. Evaluate the themes of freedom, redemption and hope in this story as they have helped define who you are.

11. How would you compare those who helped and housed the Pedro Pan children with those who helped the children in Nazi Germany? What do you think Cuban and German police forces had in common? Would such a police state be possible anywhere today? Why or why not?

12. Do you enjoy novels with historical backgrounds? Did you learn much about Cuba's history and the Cuba/U.S. relationship through this story?

13. Can you relate to the parents' decision to send their children abroad, despite the personal sacrifice? Do you understand a love so strong that they were willing to lose them in order to save them?

14. How do you think most people determine what kind of life is worth living? How have you determined that for yourself? How did it affect your life choices and decisions?

RESOURCES

Primary Sources

Cuban Heritage Collection at the University of Miami.

Walsh, Bryan, *Monsignor Bryan O. Walsh Papers,* Barry University Archives and Special Collections, Miami Shores, Florida. Scope: 1948-2001, pub. 2010.

Secondary Sources

Aschkenas, Lea & Maret, Susan, *Operation Pedro Pan: The Hidden History of 14,000 Cuban Children,* Emerald Group Publishing, 2011.

Cleeton, Chanel, *Next Year in Havana,* Berkley, CA. LLC, Penquin-Random House, 2018.

Conde, Yvonne M., *Operation Pedro Pan: The Untold Exodus of 14,048 Cuban Children,* New York, N.Y., Routledge, 1999.

Eire, Carlos, *Learning to Die in Miami: Confessions of a Refugee Boy,* New York, N.Y., Free Press, 2011.

Eire, Carlos, *Waiting for Snow in Havana: Confessions of a Cuban Boy,* New York, N.Y., Free Press, 2003.

Gonzalez, Christina Diaz, *The Red Umbrella,* New York, N.Y., Yearling, 2010.

Martínez, Lorenzo Pablo, *Cuba Adiós: A Young Man's Journey to Freedom,* Lorenzo Pablo Martínez, 2014.

Miami Dade College's Cuban Legacy Gallery at the Freedom Tower.

Torres, María de los Angeles, *The Lost Apple: Operation Pedro Pan—Cuban Children in the United States, and the Promise of a Better Future*, Boston, Mass., Beacon Press, 2003.

Triay, Victor Andrés, *Fleeing Castro: Operation Pedro Pan and the Cuban Children's Program*, Miami, FL., University Press of Florida, 1998.

Vidal, Guillermo Vicente, *Boxing for Cuba: An Immigrant's Story*, Colorado, Fulcrum Publishing, 2007.

Blogs, Magazine and Newspaper Articles

Anderson, Maria, Smithsonian Insider, *Pedro Pan: A Children's Exodus from Cuba*, July 11, 2017

Cauce, Rita M., *Operation Pedro Pan: 50 Years Later*, www.//digitalcommonsfiu.edu/gloovks/38

Historical Overview-Operation Pedro Pan/Cuban Children's Program, LibGuides at Barry University.

NPR, *Children of Cuba Remember Their Flight to America*.

Operation Peter Pan Blog: *¿Como fué?* www.//smci-colorado.edu/guillermo/index.php./peterpan/

Operation Pedro Pan Collections Guide/University of Miami Libraries

Quadrivium: A Journal of Multi-disciplinary Scholarship. Vol 6, Issue 1, Art. 3, 2014.

Schiffer, Kathy, *National Catholic Register*:
www.ncregister/com/blog/kschiffer/how-the-catholic-
church-rescued-14,000-children-from-fidel-castro.

The Voice-Weekly Publication of the Diocese of Miami
Covering the 16 Counties of South Florida, October 5,
1962.

The Key-Sketches of the 8 Newly Appointed Monsignori by
Msgr. Michael Beerhelter, Miami, FL. Dec. 21, 1963

Internet Articles

www.bishop-accountability-org/news5/2001/03/01/Walsh
History.

www.ducksters.com/history/cold_war/Cuban_missle_
crisis.php. "The Cold War for Kids: Cuban Missile
Crisis."

www.//eguides.barry.edu/c.php?g=754119&p=5403148.

www.//en.wikipedia.org/wiki/Operation_Peter_Pan.

www.//en.wikipedia.org/wiki/Cuban_Missile_Crisis.

www.insider.si.edu/2017/07/pedro-pan-childrens-
exodus-cuba.

www.//ncregister.com/blog/kschiffer/how-the-Catholic-
Church-rescued-1400-children-from-fidel_Castro.

www.//news-nationalgeographic.com/2015/08/150814-
cuba-operation-peter-pan-embassy-reopening-Castro/

www.//orlandodiocese.org/e-scroll/archive/new-pedro-
pan-documentary-debuts-in-central-florida

ABOUT THE ARTIST

Combining her mutual love of photography and history, Gini Steele and her husband Richard have created an extensive collection of photographic images of times long gone by. Throughout their work with historical societies, archivists and researchers they realized that there was a need to restore and reproduce these  historic images and make them available before they are lost forever.

Staying true to the genre, Ms. Steele used traditional photographic processes to both restore and reproduce the collection of old glass plates, negatives and photographs. She enjoys the challenge of interpreting the old negatives in her darkroom and prints the silver gelatin photographs by hand one at a time. Once the photographs are printed, they are tinted by hand. Once the hand-tinting is accomplished, Gini uses digital technology to complete the image, creating a unique piece of art.

Gini resides in Beaufort, SC with her two cats Bailey and Penelope Butterbeans.